STILL BITTER

STILL BITTER

VICK BREEDY

TABLE OF CONTENTS:

ACKNOWLEDGEMENTS:

Thank you God. Thank you Team Bitter for your unconditional support. Thank you to anyone that has read Bitter and took a moment to let me know how much you enjoyed it. That motivated me to write this sequel.

DEDICATION:

I dedicate this sequel to my grandfather "Pa." You always told me that you saw me doing something greater than the typical nine-to-five. You were right. I love you and I miss you.

STILL BITTER

Bitter Offspring

Karma:

Mom taught me that there is power between my legs. She said that every woman has it, but not every woman knows how to market it. She said that a woman has to make sure her outer package makes men want to find out just how much power she has between her legs. So, being fat was not an option for me.

One year my size-four frame went to a size six. No big deal, right? Wrong. My mom acted as if I was disrespecting her by gaining weight. She cussed me out like I'd never been cussed out before. My mom has two sides to her. She can be caring, loving and empathetic one moment and the next moment she's talking to you like you shit on her new bed sheets.

I learned at an early age to take what she said seriously. So, today, I'm in the gym. I'm on the treadmill farthest from the door so that I'm not distracted by people coming in and out of the gym. Of course I look sexy. I'm wearing a v-cut hot-pink sports bra and black Lycra shorts that might as well be panties. That's how short they are. My hair is on the top of my head in a bun. I have on waterproof mascara and Dior rose-colored lip gloss.

6

If I had it my way, I'd be here in a pair of basketball shorts and a t-shirt. My mother would have a fit if I came out of the house like that. She didn't care if I was going to the gym to sweat. I still had to be fly, which translates to marketing my power is a full-time job. My mom had me at the salon every week getting my hair done. She kept my hands manicured and feet pedicured. My wardrobe was always high end, along with my footwear and accessories. I felt like I was being set up to be pimped.

It was crazy! She had control over everything. She didn't want me to lose my virginity early. This is something I can totally understand. Moms are supposed to want their daughters to save it for their husbands. Moms don't want their daughters to be teenage moms. Here's where my mom differs from any other mom I know. Instead of giving me the "wait until marriage" talk, she bought me my first vibrator and told me to place it on my clit. She assured me that it will do a better job than any horny acne-faced boy could do. What do you say after that? Nothing. You say absolutely nothing. I learned to just listen and keep it moving.

Most daughters wouldn't know how to handle that type of encounter with their mom. For me, that was as common as brushing my teeth. Uncomfortable talks like that happened all the time. Although she didn't want me having sex yet, she wanted me to know all about it. She wanted me to be prepared when the time came. She taught me about giving head and swallowing. She bought me all types of books about the art of making love. My mom even supplied me with porn to go along with my toys.

As I was saying, I'm at the gym looking good and feeling good. I'm about forty minutes into my hour-long cardio routine on the treadmill and something hits me. I gasp. I immediately look to my left and to my right. There's an elderly white woman two treadmills away from me on my right. She's dressed in high water sweatpants, a dollar store baseball cap and a t-shirt that has food stains on it. Two treadmills to my left, there is another older woman. She's Hispanic. She's in a matching zip-up spandex jacket and leggings. That shit is too tight. She has to be a size fourteen and the outfit is fitting her like it's an eight.

As I'm assessing the women to my left and right, I gasp again. This time it goes into my mouth. I can taste it! One of these bitches needs to get off of the treadmill and walk their sloppy ass to the bathroom. Someone keeps farting. I would have let the first fart slide, but by the third one, I am pissed.

Everyone has experienced a fart slipping out of their ass when they least expect it to, but not three! One of these bitches is fucking up my work-out! I have to get off of the treadmill prematurely. I can't take it. I look at them to see if either of them will acknowledge the smell. Nope, neither of them do. I mean damn, how hard is it to just sit your ass on the toilet and take a shit? Spare the other unsuspecting people from their poisonous ass-hole wind!

I make a point to walk in front of both of their treadmills and give them dirty looks. Then, I head over to the free weights. I spend the next hour working on my arms, shoulders and back. Tomorrow, I'll work on my legs and abs. I'm in this gym five days a week for two hours. My mom insists that I get a two-hour workout to maintain my physique.

I'm built just like my mom. We are the same size, same height, same light eyes and light hair. Although, she's almost thirty years older than me, she could give me a run for my money from the neck down. Unfortunately, her face can't compete.

8

The year that I was born, my crazy vindictive father splashed battery acid in her face causing it to be disfigured. My mom has had multiple surgeries to fix her face. She no longer looks like the guy from the movie Mask. Now she looks like a woman that has had too many face lifts. Her face looks super tight and her skin texture resembles plastic. She doesn't even look related to me. I look like my dad, but I'm built like my mom. She told me that she never met her dad, but her mom told her that she looked like him and she was built like her. I guess it runs in the family.

The face she has now is the only face I've ever known. I was too young to actually remember when her faced was disfigured. I saw lots of pictures though. I feel badly for her. I know that she was once so beautiful. I heard stories about how all the girls in the neighborhood couldn't stand her because she was so pretty. If I was my mom, I probably would have wanted to kill myself after the acid incident. I mean she puts so much emphasis on beauty and being marketable. I don't know how she dealt with going from a face like Beyoncé to a face like Joan Rivers.

My mom said that it all worked out for the best. She said because she became disfigured by my father, she was able to provide a more-than-comfortable life for us. She was convinced that her suffering turned out to be beneficial for us. When I was old enough to understand, I figured out what she meant by that.

My mom had surveillance devices in her home when it happened. The entire incident was caught on tape. She blackmailed my father into keeping her bank account stacked on top of the healthy child support she got for eighteen years. If he didn't pay, she threatened to have his ass locked under the jail and then let Craig handle him. He must have believed her, because we have a lot of money. Happy birthday to me!

Ben:

Almost twenty years later, after finishing up with the child support a year ago, I'm still paying Ava. The only reason why I haven't killed her is because if the tape ever got out, it wouldn't take long for the police to connect and charge me with her murder. I hate that hoe. She is an evil bitch. I really think something is wrong with her.

After I fucked up her face, this crazy bitch had the nerve to take close-up pictures of her face and have someone decorate my bedroom walls them. They were poster-size pictures. They shocked and scared the shit out of me. That's some sick, psychotic shit. Her cousin Craig is just as crazy. So, I just pay her every month. I'm ruthless, but they've got me beat in the crazy department.

As I've aged, I've calmed down a lot. I try to let the young guys handle all of the ripping and running while I delegate. Craig doesn't know that I am a patient and calculating man. He will soon find out the power of a man that has those traits.

Craig:

As much as Ava pleaded with me to let things go, I couldn't. I held true to my word. Ben's family was on my personal hit list. I usually had other people do my dirty work, but this was something I needed to do. I killed Charlene. I killed Brian and his new family. The only member of Ben's immediate family that I didn't kill was his daughter Evelyn. I had one of my main bitches kidnap the baby and take her down south to be raised by one of her relatives. I was a day away from killing Ben and that's when Ava convinced me not to.

To this day, I still feel like I should have killed that arrogant motherfucker. Twenty years ago, Ava convinced me that it was in her best interest to have him around. She said she wanted a good life. Ben would have no choice but to provide it for her. He'd be no good to her dead. She said that she wanted Karma to know her daddy. Ava never knew hers.

Ava didn't shed a tear when she found out that Brian and his new family were no longer breathing. She broke down when she found out that Charlene had been killed. She didn't question me about it, but she did say that they had just squashed their beef. Ava said that she was looking forward to having a friendship with her again. I've known Charlene since she was in high school. That still didn't stop me from killing her. She married the wrong man. She should have stayed with that broke dude Derek. At least she would still be alive.

When all of this went down, word on the street was that Ben was talking all kinds of shit. He was telling people that whoever was responsible for all the killings was going to do

11

more than pay. Once I heard this, I made a surprise visit to his home and gave him the worst

beat down of his life! Ava didn't want him dead, but she said nothing about teaching him a

lesson. At that point, I didn't have to tell him that I was the person that killed his family. He

knew. I promised him that the only person keeping him alive right now was Ava. I would have

killed him after I let him watch me murder his wife.

Needless to say, the shit-talking stopped. Ben never fucked with Ava again and he made

sure that Ava's bank account was stacked. I told him that he better double whatever it was that

she asked for. Since then, Ava and Karma never had a broke day.

People make me out to be this bad guy, but I'm really not as bad as they say. I have a

few rules that I live by. Rule number one: Don't fuck with my family. Do so and I will wipe out

your bloodline. Rule number two: If it don't make money, it don't make sense. I'm all about

making money. If you ain't making none, you ain't in my circle. Rule number three: Stay loyal. If

you are loyal to me, I will remain loyal to you (with the exception of bitches). Show me that you

are disloyal and I become a monster.

Ava:

God sure hasn't lost his sense of humor. Before the battery acid incident, my beauty was

the cause of a lot of emotional pain. My mom couldn't deal with my beauty. The girls from

school couldn't deal with my beauty. Now I'm ugly and I can't deal with my lack of beauty.

I've had several plastic surgeries to reconstruct my face. I no longer look disfigured, but my face still looks a little off. I'm done with the surgeries. It is what it is now. This is the face I will have for the next phase of my life.

My daughter Karma has grown up to be a beautiful woman. I want her to have everything that I never had. I want her to be the woman that I could never be. I don't want her to be hurt the way that I was. I don't want her to be tormented because of her beauty like I was. I've taught her to embrace it and most importantly, to capitalize on it.

I taught her everything that my mom taught me and everything that she failed to teach me. As a result, Karma is tough cookie. She thinks I'm too hard on her and that I'm controlling. I am hard on her. I am controlling. She just doesn't know that it's for her own good. She'll appreciate how I raised her when she has her own daughter one day.

Getting back to God's sense of humor, when Karma was two, my mother found herself a preacher dumb enough to marry her. She claimed that she was saved and acts like a holy roller today. She's as fake as they come. I know her core. She's an evil bitch. She is putting up a front. She's not saved and she's not fooling me.

Don't get me wrong. It has been over fifteen years since she's been married to the preacher. They had a huge church and congregation of about five thousand members. She was the First Lady. Let her tell it she was just as important as Oprah. Well, all of that ended when her husband got arrested for embezzlement. He's in jail for the next ten years. You might as well call that a death sentence because he is seventy-years-old.

She was left with nothing at age sixty-nine. She lost everything and now she's living with me. My mother guilt-tripped me into allowing her to stay with me. She talked about how she was there for me when my face was all fucked up. She *was* there, but I didn't ask her or want her to be. She just stressed me out more.

She was the last person I wanted to go through that ordeal with. At that time, my mental health state was questionable. She came up every weekend for about two months to help out. Her helping out was more like her getting in the way. Thank God for Lance. He stayed with me for six months and nursed me back to health. He did so much for me I felt like I owed him some pussy, but I know he doesn't get down like that. He prefers dick. Instead, when I got my first check from Ben, I gave Lance half. He tried to not accept it, but I insisted.

Little did I know, Lance took the money and opened up a savings account for Karma. He said that it could be for college or for her future wedding. I told him that Ben would take care of college. He told me that he would pay for his niece's wedding then. He was such a good man. We would have been perfect for each other if he liked women. On his birthday, I bought him a black 760 BMW. The one that *I'd* always wanted.

Lance was super excited when I pulled up to his house one Sunday morning in it. He thought that I had finally gotten it for myself. He was speechless when I handed him the remote to his car. The car had a keyless entry. I had his license plates personalized. The plate read BDLANCE.

After about ten seconds of silence, he screamed at the top of his lungs and gave me the best hug I've ever gotten in my life. He was crying because he thought the license plate was

14

hilarious. He said that knowing me, I tried to make the license plate say BIGDICK, but settled for BDLANCE when the registry of motor vehicles turned it down. He knew me like a book. That was exactly what happened. The lady at the registry thought I'd lost my mind and couldn't believe I had the audacity to request such a distasteful thing. She obviously didn't know me.

Making Lance happy made me happy. He was the closest thing to family that I had outside of Craig. I started crying with him. I was crying because I was happy I could show someone I loved just how much they meant to me and know in my heart that they loved me back. That was a very special day for me.

Lance is married now. He treats his husband like a king and his husband reciprocates. They are such a cute couple. They've been talking about adopting. Lance is on the fence about it because he doesn't think an adoption agency would give a black and Dominican gay couple a child. I told him that he is being paranoid and encouraged him to go through with the process. He took my advice and is waiting on the adoption agency to get back to him. I can't wait to be an aunty.

Eve:

I never graduated from high school. Gina needed me to help with the bills. Going to school wasn't putting any food on the table. So I dropped out. I struggled in school anyway. The

15

teachers made me feel like shit whenever I got the wrong answer or when I did poorly on a test. The girls that I chilled with at school were no help when it came to book smarts. We all ended up dropping out in the eleventh grade.

My mother, Gina, got me a job where she worked at the Super Wal-Mart. We both worked as cashiers. Two small paychecks were better than one. I couldn't see myself working there for too long. I had to put up with too much bullshit working there. People were so ignorant and rude.

During my first week as a cashier, one lady came into my twelve-items-or-less line with at least twenty-five items. I told her that my line was for customers with a lot-less items. This rude-ass lady had the nerve to say, "Look you little bitch, just ring up my shit before I get your manager." I started to tell her to go ahead and call my manager. My mother was in the next line ringing up a customer and giving me the evil eye at the same time. She looked at me like I'd be taking money out of her pocket for giving that lady a hard time.

I sucked my teeth and rang all thirty of that bitch's items up. Once it was time for her to pay, her credit card didn't even approve her balance. She huffed and puffed as if I was taking too long. The problem was her card. It had nothing to do with me being a new cashier. Her shit kept declining. I tried to be polite and ask her if she had another card that she'd like to use. She said no and started telling me which items to put back and which ones to ring up again. I was heated!

I was way-past pissed. The heifer was holding up the twelve-items-or-less line with her bullshit. I had to end up calling a manager to void out the transaction. When he asked why there were so many items to void, the bitch answered for me and said that she didn't realize

that this line was for twelve items or less. She had the nerve to lie and say that she would have

moved to the other line if I told her that she was in the wrong line.

I figured that she lied because my manager is white. It kills me how black people can talk

a lot of shit to a black employee, but when someone white shows up on the scene they change

their attitude with the quickness. Why do black people do each other this way? All that mouth

she had before was gone. In the end, she bought about eight items and had the nerve to try to

rush me after all of her items were voided. People in line were putting their items down and

walking out of the store. I didn't blame them. If I could have left, I would have too.

When my shift was over, I didn't go home. I took the bus to my girl's house. I was beat

and I just wanted to chill. I couldn't believe that I had to work on my birthday. Lynn didn't work.

She braided hair when she needed some extra cash. Lynn's boyfriend bought her whatever she

wanted whenever she wanted. The only time that she didn't have money was when she was

mad at him. She wouldn't swallow her pride and ask him for money. She'd just find someone

that needed their hair braided.

I knew that Lynn would be home. If she wasn't out with me during the day, she was at

home. Her man did most of his business during the day. He only came to see Lynn at night.

Therefore, I didn't need to call and check to see if she would be home.

I got to her door and I could smell the weed through the door. I knocked on the door

and she yelled that the door was open. This chick never locked her door. She said that nobody

had enough balls to rob her because of who her man was. That sounded crazy to me. There

17

were so many crack heads in the area. When they are feigning, they don't care who her man is. She should know by now that a crack head has no conscience.

Lynn was smoking weed and surfing the net for Christian Louboutin shoes. She was definitely a whore when it came to buying named brand shoes. I told her that nobody around our way could tell the difference between high end shoes and those from Marshalls. Lynn didn't care. That was her thing. She used to joke and say if she had to choose between dick and shoes, shoes would always win. She said that they usually stick around longer. She had a point.

I don't smoke weed. She was considerate enough to put it out once I entered the living room. Lynn is one of the prettiest females that I know. She reminds me of a Nia Long. She's looks just like her except she's tall. Lynn is six feet. She could be a super model. She has a C cup with a small waist and round booty. She would be a designer's dream, but instead she's a drug dealers boo.

Ben:

It's sixty degrees outside and it's October. Sixty in October feels like summer in Massachusetts. The day was going pretty well until I remembered what the day was. Karma's and Evelyn's birthday is today. I really wish that they could have gotten a chance to know each other. I don't even know if Ava ever told Karma that she had a sister that was killed.

I'm driving down Melnea Cass in Roxbury and come to a red light. I'm in the left lane because I'm trying to take that cut-through street to Blue Hill. I have my windows down and my music blasting. This tall, skinny, dark-skinned dude that looks to be about my age has a bucket out and offers to clean the windows of my Benz. He wants to clean it with some dirty ass brown water. I tell the piece of shit that if he gets a drop of that nasty ass water on my whip that I will jump out the car and punch the teeth that he has left out of his mouth. I can't stand these weak motherfuckers. Get a job or get a bitch to take care of you. Be a man!

Ava:

The day is sunny. It's warmer than it should be for October. I turn on the radio to listen to NPR and catch up with current events. I have the windows down. The breeze feels good. I wish that I didn't have my wig on so that my scalp could feel the breeze. My hair's been getting thin. I've been wearing a wig every day for the past four months. I'm half listening to NPR and find myself daydreaming. I scare myself because I don't remember driving the last mile or so. I have a lot on my mind.

I stopped working after Ben threw battery acid in my face. That was right after Karma was born. The payment arrangement that I have with Ben has allowed me to not have to work. The more money that he gives me, the more money I invest. I've made smart investments. I really don't need any more money from Ben, but I still take it. I feel like he owes it to me.

Now that Karma is grown, she's at the house less. I wish that I could say the same for my mother. I've offered to get her a place to live, but she insists on staying with me. I've come right out and asked her when she's leaving. Her response is usually something smart-mouthed or passive aggressive. As much as she complains, it's never bad enough for her to pack up her shit and leave.

Most of the time, I just tune her out. If I pay her too much attention, she'll make me say something to her ass that she won't like. In the meantime, I need to find something to do. I have been thinking about starting a business, but I may need some of my cousin's connections to bring it to fruition. That's what I was daydreaming about when I lost a mile driving.

I'm slowly approaching a red light and notice a few dragonflies zipping around. I quickly try to roll up my windows, but I'm not quick enough. One of those bastards flies in the car with me. I go straight into panic mode! What are dragonflies doing out in October? The light turns green, but I can't move. I've been in shock for about five seconds. The car behind me is blowing his horn. I rip my thumb nail from my skin trying to get out of my seatbelt. Once I release it, I jump out of the car.

There's no way that I'm getting back into that car. I'm in the middle of Warren Street, in Roxbury, scared for my life. I'm not afraid of being alone on Warren Street. I am afraid because a big ass dragonfly bum rushed me. I mean seriously, what are the chances of one of those bugs flying directly into a car? I feel like a fool because I let something that was small enough for me to step on jack me for my Benz. Bugs and I do not do well.

After about twenty long seconds, I walk up to my car window to see if it hopefully flew out. Just as I peek in, it flies directly into my forehead! Out of instincts, I slap my forehead. Then, I scream as I fall back and lose my balance trying to get out of its way. If I thought that I looked like a fool when I ran out of the car, I am convinced that I look far worse when I fall on my ass.

Not one person offers to help me or see what the problem is. One ignorant asshole actually drives by in his hoopty and yells, "Get the fuck out the street hoe!" I am pissed! Folks are more concerned about me blocking traffic than anything else. Ava, twenty years ago, would have taken off her shoe and thrown it at whoever was bold enough to talk trash while she was having a weak moment. Ava, today, has gotten good at controlling her rage. I'm good, but not cured.

One moment I'm daydreaming about my next business plan and the next moment I'm on my ass on Warren Street. Traumatized, I get back into my car, roll up my windows and put the air conditioner on. There will be no repeats of tonight ever again. Thank God I was at a red light. If I had been driving, I definitely would have crashed the car trying to get away from a bug. Once I am in my car, safe and sound, my thumb starts to throb. I call Craig and ask him to meet me at one of our old spots later on tonight. I have a business plan I want to run past him.

Karma:

I am trying my best to practice celibacy. I am not waiting until marriage. I am basically

waiting for the highest bidder. I know that sounds tasteless, maybe even whorish, but nobody

was getting my power—as my mom and I like to call it—for free. Last Friday night, I almost

broke my celibacy. I was a cross between drunk and high. I usually don't allow myself to get

tore up, but I was.

I met this guy named Bradley at Darryl's, a club on Columbus Ave. in the South End. He

was saying all of the right things and he was sexy as hell. We danced to a few Reggae songs and

it was over after that. I had been drinking beer and Hennessey. Then someone put me on to

Molly. I took some and Molly had me all hot and bothered. I'd never had sex, but after taking

that Molly shit I was ready to fuck.

Bradley almost got it Friday night. He walked me to my car. I was so twisted that he

offered to drive me home. I had enough sense to tell him that I wasn't leaving my Benz out

there overnight and jumping into a car with a man that I just met. Instead, my dumb ass let him

drive me home in my car. He had his boy follow him in his car.

Once we pulled up into my driveway he started talking all types of nasty shit to me, the

type of freaky stuff that I like. Molly had me thirsty for the dick. One minute he was telling me

about his skills in the pussy-eating department and the next minute, I had him proving it right in

front of my house.

When I say it was the best I've ever had, I am not lying. I would go to church and testify

on it! It was so good that I almost let him convince me to let him "just put the tip in." Those are

his words, not mine. That Molly and Hennessey mix almost had me lose my virginity. I promised

myself that I wouldn't mess with that Molly bitch again. She plays with your head too much.

Had he tried a little harder for a little while longer, I might have fucked him and his boy.

The next morning I woke up craving dick. My dream was intense. It was about that dude

Bradley. *He is in my house and nobody is here but us two. I want him to come to the bedroom,*

but he says he likes to eat at the dining room table. I am confused for about three seconds. I

can't understand why he is talking about eating. By the fourth second, I understand.

Bradley strips down to nothing and puts my hand on his thick dick while he undresses

me. I massage his dick while he skillfully peels off my clothes. Once I am naked, he picks me up

and places me on the dining room table. He spreads my legs and admires my pretty pussy. Then

he goes to work! It is better than what he did in the car. Every lick has me jumping. Each lick

feels like long overdue relief. He is nursing my pussy to back sexual health. Then he gives it one

long wet lick and without warning he thrusts his big dick inside of me. I gasp and I wake up!

When I awake, I am seriously thinking about calling him. If he can do that shit to me in

my dream, I may need to experience what he can do to me in person. I grab my vibrator to take

the edge off a little. I may need to investigate how deep his pockets go.

Ben:

Once I finish with my business on Blue Hill, I drive down to Slade's to eat some fried chicken and look at the young-hood bitches that come in here. Now, don't get me wrong, some of the chicks that go into Slade's are fine as hell. They got big-juicy-project booties. They dress like they are cast members on Basketball Wives. The problem is that they got a hood mentality.

They want a man that has a nice car, nice home and a fat pocket. The type of bitch that I am looking for, I'm not gonna find at Slade's. I want the bitch that doesn't require a man to take care of her better than she can take care of herself. With that being said, this type of bitch has her own money, is educated, in shape and is not opposed to sucking dick. I want a bitch that doesn't need me. I want one that "wants" me. That way, it will make our relationship all about the love, because that's all we need from each other.

Speaking of bitches, Craig has a new bitch. I've had eyes on Craig ever since he stole on me in my home years ago. A lot of time has gone by, but I haven't forgotten or forgiven him for that foul shit. I vowed that I would get him back in a way that really hit home. I knew that if I killed Ava, it would hit him hard, but I couldn't kill Ava. I didn't want to be linked to her murder or investigated for it. My patience has paid off. I got a plan to really fuck his head up. Pay back is a bitch and a bitch will be the payback!

Getting back to me and finding a lady, it's not gonna happen at Slade's. Tonight I'm not looking for a lady. I want someone I can impress with a few dollars thrown at them and get some head. I'm looking for a hoe that doesn't know she's a hoe. I want someone that will be impressed with my Benz and the three-hundred dollar bottle that I will buy for her and her girls' table. I will admit that I miss Ava. She had that serious head game. To this day, I haven't met anyone that could beat or match her. Believe me, I've been interviewing.

I've had my eyes on her too over the years. Both she and her cousin Craig have been under surveillance. She's living pretty comfortably, courtesy of me. That battery acid really did a number on her. She's gotten a few cosmetic procedures on her face and she looks nothing like the Ava I used to sweat. In the face, she looks like Joan Rivers' tanned sister. No joke. I almost feel bad for her, but she's living life real good right now. That battery acid incident worked out in her favor in the end. The bitch should send me a thank you card! That shit is funny as hell to me.

It's one a.m. and my project booty and her girls have finished the bottle I sent over to them. She's left her girls and is sitting at my table grinning all up in my face. She's nice right now. I ask her if she wants to come over and have a night cap and smoke some weed. She's down. Her name is Jackie. Jackie is eager to go home with me. I have no plans of taking her to my crib. Can't have these bitches knowing where I rest my head at. So I take her to the Marriott.

I must say, she impresses me, but her head game is weak and she won't swallow. If your head game is weak, at least make up for it by swallowing. I mean damn, what's a brother gotta do to get bitches to swallow nowadays? Jackie is gonna need to step her game up big time,

25

especially if she wants to roll with me from time to time. That booty is working in her favor

though. I just might consider training her to please Big Ben the way he requires to be pleased.

Eve.

I met my new man at a club called Tempo in Charlotte. Club nights at Tempo were the

best. They changed the name of this club so many times over the years, but finally decided to

give it the name it had back when my mother Gina was my age and clubbing. Nobody ever

called it any of the names that they changed it to. They couldn't make the new names stick. We

never stopped calling it Tempo.

My new man Richard and I have been going strong for about two months now. I broke

up with my last boyfriend because I found out he was fucking some other bitch from work. She

knew that he was my man. That's why I can't stand bitches. If she didn't know, then I wouldn't

blame her at all. But that bitch knew. She worked with him and she saw me more than a few

times with him.

She is a thirsty bitch. I've been told that she let him do it to her in her car during their

lunch break. I have nothing against doing it in your car, but not with someone that you know

has no intentions of being with you. You are the jump off that he can get a quickie from and

then he go home to his woman. Some women don't care, but I'm not the one. I have a friend that works with my ex-boyfriend Vince. I never told him this because I wanted to have someone watching him without him knowing.

I found out by my friend that he was doing the bitch on his lunch breaks. She took pictures on her phone and sent them to me. To say I was shocked is an understatement. I thought for sure that my man was loyal to me. I was loyal to him. Best believe I had dudes checking for me all the time. I passed up plenty of dick for Vince and look what he does to me in return. Bitches! Yes, he is a bitch. I use the term loosely for men and women.

My new man Richard has been great. My only complaint is that he is busy as hell. But honestly, I rather him be busy than stalking my every move. The first time we were together, I couldn't walk without discomfort for two days. I joke and call him "Mr. Put It Down and Shut It Down." He does his job soooo good. Then he makes sure I can't get none from anybody else because my pussy needs to recover. Correction: his pussy needs to recover. My pussy is no longer mine. Richard got it on lock. I told him that he got me dickmatized. He asked what that meant. I told him that he got my coochie under a powerful spell!

Despite the rough sex "issue", this is the best sex I've had. He makes me feel comfortable. He encourages me to ask for "whatever" I want and he will make it happen. I don't feel like a hoe. I feel cherished and valued when we have sex. Don't get me wrong, we do some freaky-ass shit. You might consider it closer to fucking than love-making, yet it is still meaningful. We are connecting sexually and emotionally.

This last episode took me for a loop. I almost didn't know how to take it. As he was eating me, he spit on my pussy. I said to myself, "*Should I feel disrespected?*" I had never had

27

anyone purposely spit on it. I don't know. Everything is different with him. Not only did I not feel disrespected. I got turned on even more. I liked that shit. It's funny because now I order him to spit on it and then lick it up. I can see myself falling for this man hard, but I can't let him know just how hard I have the potential to fall.

Richard is fine as hell. He's just my type, basketball-player height and build, dark skin, straight teeth, sexy lips and a strong dick. I hope things work out between us because my coochie has gotten spoiled. She doesn't want to let her new friend go and she definitely doesn't want to find out that she's been sharing him with someone else. That will be a serious problem for all parties involved.

Richard and I are supposed to meet at Tempo tonight. I ask Lynn to come with me, because I know Rich won't be there until close to midnight. If I'm gonna spend my hard-earned money to get into the club, I'm gonna get my money's worth. I am not going to show up late. I don't work three jobs like Richard. I need to be there before eleven p.m. I need to secure the spot that I am gonna be posing at all night. Lynn's always down to pose with me at the club. She says, "Let the females hate and the fellas salivate." Her height alone gets her a lot of attention.

I call Lynn and ask her to meet me at Tempo's parking lot around ten thirty p.m. She says she can't go tonight. I'm like *"what?"* She said that her man needs her to do something for him tonight. She doesn't know when she will be done. This is the part about our friendship that I can't stand. She's dating a drug dealer and I'm always worried about her. I know that she does "things" for him. I just don't want to see her getting caught up behind his bullshit.

I tell her, "Ok", and promise to fill her in on all of the shit that goes down at the club when we talk tomorrow. She blows me a kiss through the phone and commands me to "Let the females hate and the fellas salivate!" I blow her a kiss back and tell her, "You already know!"

I get to the club around eleven p.m. As expected, Richard isn't here yet. I case the place for a spot to stand at that is not too far from the entrance and open enough to be seen by all. I get my drink and then post up at my spot for the night. I already see bitches giving me the evil eye. That confirms that my shit's on point. So, thank you bitches. I also see a couple of fellas undressing me with their eyes. I pull out my phone and text Lynn: MISSION COMPLETE: BITCHES ARE HATING AND FELLAS ARE SALIVATING! LOL!

I have on a hot pink spandex mini dress that fits every curve with precision. The dress looks like a second skin, but in a good way, not a trashy way. I have on some of Lynn's shoes that I borrowed and never gave back to her. I don't remember the designer's name, but they are violet high heels and fly as hell. All of Lynn's shoes are eye-catching and expensive.

My looks don't favor my mom on any level. She told me that I look just like my dad, as if he spit me out himself. I have dark-brown eyes, dark-brown hair that I dye blonde, I'm five feet seven inches and curvy. These heels got me measuring in at about six feet tonight.

The latest Rick Ross comes on and I find myself doing the MJB bounce with my head down and my hand in the air. Rick Ross is not my type in the looks department, but his songs keep me dancing. He's been making hits for twenty years now.

I look up and this dude is standing in front of me smiling. I'm a little caught off guard because I am so busy jamming, I didn't realize he was there. My first instinct is to put on my

29

irritated face and ask if I can help him with something; which I do. This dude says "no" and

keeps standing there. I look at my watch. It's only eleven thirty p.m. Rich will be here like

clockwork at midnight. So, if I want to flirt a little bit, I can. This dude is a cutie and is cocky as

hell. That's just how I like them. The only difference is that this time around, my flirting would

be limited. He is fine and all, but Richard is fine, too, and has my heart. Being fine isn't going to

make a relationship last. Shit most of the time it's what gets a relationship into trouble.

Someone starts feeling themselves too much and then the trouble starts.

Anyway, this cutie is standing in front of me looking all cocky like, "You know you want

me." I ask him how long he's gonna stand there looking stupid. He laughs and says nothing. The

dude just stands there. I start to get a little weirded out by this. Finally, he says, "So, what's up

with you? You wanna dance?'

"No, thanks."

"Why not? You over here dancing hard to Rick Ross like you want to get on the dance

floor."

"I already have a dance partner and he's on his way."

"Oh, so that's how it is? What you married? You can't dance with anyone else."

"Oh, honey, don't get it twisted. I can dance with anyone that I want. I just only want to

dance with my man. And you aren't him. So fall back."

"DAMNNNNN! It's like that?"

"Yes, it's like that."

"Aight, Bitch. Kick rocks then."

Just as I am about to cuss the dude out, Richard punches him in the face and takes me over to a table to sit down. He acts like he didn't just punch a dude in his face. He doesn't get kicked out of the club either. He definitely must know someone in the club because Tempo's management doesn't play that. If you fight, both of y'all are getting thrown out.

Come to find out, as I was jamming to Rick Ross, that dude wasn't the only one watching me. Richard came to the club early and stood back to watch what was transpiring. Thank God, I had good sense to remember I had a good man in my corner. If I hadn't, that situation could've gone to the left real quick. You never know who is watching.

Richard tells me that I look pretty in my pink dress and purple heels. Then he gets up to get me a drink. As soon as he gets up, I text Lynn and tell her that I already got shit to tell her and the night ain't over. She texts me back: SMH.

The rest of the night was good. I danced for at least an hour with Richard. My feet were killing me by the time the club got out. I had to limp to my car. Richard saw this and carried me. I am really feeling this man. Bigtime!

After the club, I expected Rich to invite me to his place. Much to my disappointment, he didn't. He said he had some business to handle with his night job. We never really discussed the details of his "night job", but he said he promotes for clubs. I took his word for it. Shit, most

31

dudes around my way have a hard time holding down one job. This man has three. One is full time. The other two are part-time gigs.

Coming from my previous relationship, it is a struggle to give him the benefit of the doubt. I mean, my last dude was getting it in at work. Richard is telling me he got business to handle at two in the morning. That's hard to swallow and harder to believe. I gotta believe him though. He has done nothing to me that would warrant a lack of trust from me. He didn't do it. My ex did. That's who can't be trusted. Richard is a good man.

So, I call Lynn and see what she's doing. She's still out with her boo. I decide to bring my ass home and go to sleep. I really want to hang, but my silly behind knows that I have to get up early to be at Wal-Mart. I really need a new job. I gotta get out of my mother's house. I'm just not sure how I'm gonna pull it off.

My pay at Wal-Mart won't give me enough to rent an apartment that would suit me. Even if I worked overtime, I may be able to afford the apartment, but not a car note, car insurance, utilities, cell phone, food to eat and gas for my car. I am definitely going to use my lunch break to look for another job. Very different from my ex. He uses his lunch breaks to look for coochie. He got his though.

Vince lost his job after that. They both did. I sent that picture from my friend's phone straight to HR. I knew that had to be breaking some sort of company policy. I mean they were still on company property when they were fucking. He got fired. She got fired. And then I had my friend send me the email address of the nosiest, gossiping co-worker. I "accidently" sent the picture to her. I knew that it would spread like wildfire. I was right; it did. My home girl

texted me: GIRL, SHIT IS CRAZY HERE AT WORK.

Craig:

Never thought that I would settle down, but Cynthia got ya boy really considering it.

She's nothing like these tricks I've dealt with. She got a few degrees. She has her own shit. She's

sexy, but not in a flashy way. She knows when to be quiet and when to speak up. Cynthia makes

me wanna be a better man. No bitch, excuse me, no chick has ever made me feel that way. She

even has me thinking about my word choice.

I've been calling females "bitches" for as long as I could pronounce the word. Cynthia

ain't trying to hear it. I can't say "bitch" in her presence. She had the balls to say that she'd

prefer if I got out of the habit of referring to women in such a derogatory way altogether. Since

the sex is good, I decided to respect her wishes. I no longer say "bitch" in her presence. When

she's out of earshot, I still use it. It's gonna take more than good pussy to make me erase it

from my vocabulary. I'll give it to her. She succeeded in making me conscious of it though.

Cynthia and I been with each other for over a year now. Shit has been real good. I got no

complaints. I mean, she does some things that drive me a little crazy, but it ain't shit that I can't

get past. She's punctual and expects me to be the same. She's structured and tries to run our relationship like she's running a residential program. We got dates and times for everything.

Now, I'm a business man. I understand the need for structure. I want structure in my business,

not my motherfucking love life.

She tells me that life is so unpredictable. Having structure comforts her. She needs to

plan ahead and enjoys looking forward to things. I tell her that we can look forward to things

without having a daily agenda. That shit gets irritating as hell, but that's her. I work around it

because the good definitely outweighs the bad with Cynthia. I'm a lucky dude to have her.

Those weak motherfuckers that she dealt with before didn't take the time to figure out how

she ticks. Had they done that, they would have stuck with her and wouldn't have risked losing

her.

Cynthia is a loving, caring and nurturing woman. What I like the most about her is that

she is loyal. She may be closer to the book smarts than the street smarts, but she can keep a

secret. And if you are in her circle, she will have your back like no other. I call her my bougie

ride-or-die chick. She gets a kick out of it when I call her that.

She got me getting suited up for some wedding of one of her many friends. I feel like a

professional escort. She always has some cousin or relative getting married. I swear in the last

year, I've gone to about seven weddings. That shit starts to get expensive too. Don't get me

wrong. I don't mind spending money. I just like to spend it on things that I like to do or on

people that I know. I don't know these motherfuckers. I do it though. I tag along to these

boring-ass weddings to please my lady. Like, I said, the good outweighs the bad.

After the wedding, I got shit to do. Cynthia likes to plan stuff for me and thinks she got me all day. I got things that I need to handle. I'll hate to have to break it to her because I know she's going to be disappointed. She just can't get enough of ya boy. Can you blame her?

I'm not gonna front. I'm really feeling her too. I just don't openly show it the way that she does. That doesn't mean that I don't love her because I do. I love this woman. Now, that is something that I only share with her. I'm private with my shit and especially my feelings. The only other person that has a clue to how much I care for Cynthia is my cousin Ava. We are so close that she might as well be my sister. I'll kill for Ava. Shit. I have killed for Ava.

Ava calls me up and tells me that she wants to meet with me and go over a business proposition. She knows I don't talk about shit over the phone. So we decide to meet at one of our old sub shop hangouts, Lynn House of Roast Beef. I haven't been there in about twenty years. I arrive and there she is sitting at a table with her pizza roll and small order of steak fries. She has my steak and cheese sub with catsup and mayo on toasted bread waiting for me at the table with her.

She passes me her hand sanitizer, while she gets up to get our drinks. When she comes back, I hand her back the sanitizer and ask her what's up. She tells me that she wants to start a private investigation business. I start choking on my drink because the shit sounds funny. I wait for her to tell me the real reason why she wanted to meet.

Once I realize that she is serious, I tell her to go ahead and continue her pitch. She got enough money between her investments and from Ben to do whatever she wants to do. What did she need me for? She says that she wants my approval to approach some of the girls that work for me. She says that she's gotten to know some of them pretty well and there are about three of them that she would like to train and have on her team. She says at first, it would be part time, but as business picks up she will need more of their time. This means that they won't be available to me as much as they were. Ava says that she will pay me a finder's fee for each of them and then once they go full time, she'll hit me off again with triple the finder's fee. How the tables have turned; this exchange reminds me of the time that I approached her for UMass referrals.

I'm down. I'm all for my cousin wanting to start her own business. She told me her plan and I thought that it was a good "legit" hustle. She said that she already had a name for her agency. She was so serious that she had the website domain on lock and had it trademarked. The name will be Still Bitter P.I. Agency.

Karma:

Bradley calls and asks to take me out to dinner. He says that he doesn't care where we go to eat, as long as I say yes. While he is on the other end talking about how fine I am, I am listening to the background noise. He said that he is at home, so I want to hear his home environment. I plan on seeing it later on tonight.

"Girl, that outfit you had on that night was killing them!"

Beep! Beep! Beeeeeep!

"Oh, thank you Bradley. You are making me blush."

Buuuuuuuuuuuuuuuuuzz!

"Yeah, girl, you had me thinking all types of nasty thoughts."

"Stop it Bradley," I say as I continue to halfway listen to him.

"So when you gonna let me see what you got underneath them clothes?"

Is this idiot crazy? Does he really think he's going to get me undressed with that weak game? "Bradley, slow down baby. You are being a little too aggressive. You don't want to run me off do you?"

"Yo, you got some quarters I can use for the wash homie?" a deep male voice says.

"I'm on the phone, player. Wait until I get off!" Bradley barks.

"So what were you saying, baby?"

"Oh nothing. So what time you picking me up tonight? I want to go to Legal Seafood."

"Aight, I will scoop you around eight. That good?"

"It's perfect. See you then."

What I deduced from our conversation is that this idiot lives in the hood. The horn beeping the way that it was wouldn't fly in the suburbs. He lives in an apartment building because he needs to use quarters to do laundry and because he has a buzzer instead of a bell. The person that asked for the quarters must have already been there or had a key because

Bradley didn't tell me to hold on while he opened the door. I also didn't hear him walk

anywhere to open the door. This means he has a roommate. So far, none of this was working in

his favor if he thought that he was going to get some from me. His pockets may be too light for

my pussy.

Bradley picks me up in a three series BMW. It's not a Toyota, but it's not the seven

series that I would require. When I get into the car, his boy is in the back seat. (Note to self: he

didn't get out and open my door.) I have manners. I greet his boy and I instantly recognize the

deep voice. It is the same voice that I heard over the phone earlier.

Bradley says that he has to drop off his boy in route to Legals. I say it's fine, but inside

I'm heated! How are you going to take me out on our first date and have your boy in the car?

That is so tacky. He's lucky that I'm willing to let the cards unfold before I start tripping.

We drop his boy off in the projects in Malden and then we head to Legals. I

automatically assumed that we would go to the Legals in Cambridge or Boston. This fool is

heads back to the Northshore Mall to take me to that location. At this point, I'm aggravated and

hungry. This idiot isn't getting any pussy from me. He is too motherfucking basic for me. He

needs a basic bitch. And she ain't me.

I get through dinner unimpressed but full by the time the bill comes. As expected he

pays the bill with cash. The only people that use cash nowadays are people that have bad credit

or no credit. That was his strike three. I was gonna let him eat it, but now that isn't even going

down. "Take me home."

Eve:

I'm on my lunch break and decide to check Facebook to see if I have any messages. The only message I have is from Lynn. So I hit her back. She asks how my throat is because I tell her it's been hurting since the weekend. She responds by saying that she told me to stop swallowing.

"LOL. You are so stupid"

"So, what was it that you wanted to talk to me about?"

"I just need to get this off of my chest. We are girls. We tell each other everything. So, I couldn't keep this from you."

"Stop stalling! What do you wanna tell me?"

"I let Vince eat it."

"Huh?"

"I knoooooooooooooooooow, I'm sorry. I was too drunk to turn him down."

"Are you seriously inboxing me that you let my Vince eat it?"

"I felt sooooooo bad after. I told him that you are my sister. I have to tell you."

"When did this happen?"

"Believe me, it happened "after" you guys broke up."

"Am I really reading this shit?"

39

"Damn Eve, you know under normal circumstances I wouldn't have done that!"

"Bitch, you are lucky you are typing this and not telling me to my face. I'm ready to go break a bottle and stab your ass with it! I can't believe you! We are supposed to be girls, sisters and you go and do this! You think it matters that we weren't together anymore? Men that we've dated are off limits! Do I really have to tell you that? Damn, Lynn! You fucked up!"

"Eve, I'm sorry for real. It only happened one time and that shit meant nothing. He only ate it. I didn't let him do me. I told him that I was going to tell you because I felt so guilty."

"You're a fucking hoe! Does your man know you were letting my man eat your pussy?"

"Uuuum first of all Eve, he's not your man. He waaaaaas your man. Let's not get this shit twisted! And why are you asking me that? You already know the answer. What? You thinking about telling him?"

My break is over. I log off of Facebook and head back to work with a funky attitude that wasn't there thirty minutes ago. I have a headache and my heart hurts. My heart is beating fast like I am about to get caught for stealing something. I hope that bitch dies from the suspense. I could have responded to her last message. I could have told her that I'm not that shady like some folks and I wouldn't tell her man what she is doing behind his back. I didn't though. I left her hanging. Plus, her man is crazy! He might kill her and my ex. She's even crazier for cheating on him.

As of right now, that bitch is dead to me. Whether I'm gonna fuck her up when I see her again is up for debate. She knew what she was doing when she opened her legs to someone

I've opened my legs to. The grimy bitch thinks it's ok because they didn't fuck. This bitch is always getting her pussy eaten by some dude. I never thought it would be my dude.

I think about this for the rest of my shift. As soon as I get out, I call Richard and tell him the fucked up shit that Lynn did. He wonders why I even care. I tell him I care because we are like sisters and unlike dudes, sisters don't mess with each other's men, past or present. His view is, if I'm not with him anymore that means that I'm not feeling him anymore. If I'm not feeling him anymore, I shouldn't waste any energy being mad at Lynn. Then he asks if I am sure that I'm not feeling Vince anymore.

I tell him that I no longer have any feelings for Vince, but that's not the point. The point is that there is an unwritten rule between friends. The rule is that we don't swap men. There are so many men in the world. There should be no reason to have to share them. Vince is a dog. His behavior doesn't surprise me. Lynn has some hoe-ish tendencies, but she's always been loyal. She's always had my back. She knows all my secrets, all my fears and all my hang-ups in life. She's the closest thing to having a sister. She really disappointed me.

The truth is that I'm hurt. I know that people make mistakes. People are human. Lynn isn't perfect. I just thought that some things were sacred between us. It's hard for me to accept this human flaw in Lynn. Life can really fuck with your head. I want to forgive her, but I'm mad. I'm mad that she's making me have to decide if I want to continue our friendship. Lynn is my bestie. It takes a lot of work to develop the friendship that we have or should I say had. Do I want to just throw our friendship away? I CAN'T STAND GRIMY BITCHES!!!!!!!

41

I will say this. I'm sure it wasn't worth it. I never shared that with Lynn, but Vince

couldn't eat pussy to save his life! Good thing she was drunk. Now, Richard on the other hand

could give seminars on how to eat pussy. Vince's ass needs to sign up.

Karma:

Same shit, different day. I'm at the gym, on the treadmill and suddenly have to go pee

really bad. I have five minutes left to finish, but I'm positive that I can't wait. I stop the machine

and rush to the ladies room. I have to pee so badly that I almost pee on myself trying to get to

the stall. I notice that the handicap stall is free, so I take that one. The fewer things I need to

touch the better. The handicap bathroom toilet is sensor activated. I don't have to flush the

toilet with my foot.

As I squat over the toilet, I notice that the metal lock on the door didn't fasten all the

way. I'm peeing a gallon out of my bladder and looking at the door praying that it doesn't open.

I guess my relationship with God could take some strengthening because the door slowly begins

to open. I'm too far away from the door to put my arm out to stop it from opening.

Two scrawny white girls come into the bathroom as my door is opening. I can see this

because the handicap stall is all the way at the end of the bathroom. There is a mirror that

wraps around the wall all the way to the entrance of the bathroom. So, if I look out into the mirror, I can see who is coming in. What that means is that those walking in can see me squatting over the toilet. That's what I get for using the handicap stall.

I am so fucking embarrassed, but I can't do shit about it but finish peeing. They look at me like they are disgusted and embarrassed for me at the same time. They aren't compassionate enough to ask if I need them to shut the door for me. Once we make eye contact, they look away. One of them looks back and watches me as I wipe myself. She doesn't think I see her, but I do. So, I look at her as I wipe myself an extra time and she quickly turns her head. These gay bitches are getting bold!

I am definitely out of the mood to continue with my workout. I grab my stuff from out of my locker and head out of the gym. When I get to the gym exit, I notice this fine brother coming in. Now there are lots of fine brothers at this gym. I usually try to stay focused on my work out and not the fellas, but today I may make an exception.

He walks in ignoring me. That's a hard thing to do. He goes straight to the sales office. I decide to go into the sales office too. I am definitely trying to ear hustle, but act as if I want to sign up for a personal trainer. Come to find out, he runs the joint. This is his gym. I decide to get signed up with a trainer. I pick the flamboyant homosexual dude as a trainer because I know he'll have all of the information I need. If he doesn't have it, he'll get it. Let the investigation begin!

My first training starts tonight. I'm not wasting any time. To my delight, Mr. Fine is still here. He takes off his suit jacket. All he has on is his slacks and a white V-neck t-shirt that he must have worn under his dress shirt. He is looking sexy as hell. We are only five minutes into the workout and my trainer is talking about him. Just as I expected, if he likes men the way that I do, I knew he wouldn't be able to help himself from talking about this fine specimen.

By the end of my workout, I have all of the information that I want. He doesn't just own this gym. He owns the entire chain. He isn't married. He is older than me, but only by nine years. He doesn't have any kids, which means no baby-mama drama. The only negative thing that I learn about him is that he is a workaholic. To me, that isn't negative. That just means he and I have the same passion. We like money.

Eve:

I am still feeling some type of way about Lynn. I will admit that I miss our friendship. She did some foul shit, though. I just can't tell her that there's no love lost and we can pick back up right where we left off. Earlier today, I ran it by a friend of mine who doesn't know Lynn, just to see if I was overreacting. She agreed that I wasn't overreacting. From what I could tell, this bitch was feeling herself. Lynn was posting all types of stuff on Facebook. The one post that got under my skin the most was: *Your life would be boring without me.* That's it! This hoe is gonna get her ass beat.

I call Richard and tell him what this bitch is doing. He tells me not to sweat it and to leave it alone. I'm not feeling his response. I can't just leave it alone. Now she is trying to act all bold and shit. I owe her an ass whooping. It's a done deal. Next time I see her, it's on!

Richard is leaving for a week to go to some work conference out of state. Richard is a correctional officer. He also has a few side gigs doing security. He said his dream is to open his own agency of body guards. I believe he will make it happen. He is always doing stuff to better himself. He keeps his body tight and his mind right. He's a brother with a plan. I sometimes wonder what he's doing with someone like me.

I have no five-year plan. I work at Wal-Mart. I live at home with my mother. I don't even have a one-year plan. Don't get me wrong, I'm a hard worker, but I have no direction. So, like I was saying. I have no idea what Richard is doing with me. It must be the sex because I have nothing else to offer. I need to get it together. I guess it won't hurt if I start by getting my GED.

Anyway, back to Lynn, I will see her soon. I'm going to have to start hanging with some of my "sometimes" friends. The folks I call when Lynn ain't around or can't hang. I should call my cousin Casey up and see what she has planned for the weekend. I definitely need a new person to do things with now. I had Richard, but it's not the same as having a girlfriend to do things with. Lynn really messed things up.

It's Friday night. Richard left this morning to head to his conference. Crazy cousin Casey is my partner in crime this weekend. We decide to start the weekend off at Tempo. I know that there's a chance that I might see Lynn. I give Casey a heads up that shit my jump off. She isn't even phased. She has my back regardless.

45

Tonight, I'm dressed cute, but I'm strategically dressed just in case I got to throw down up in the club. We pull up to the parking area and it is packed as usual. Casey was late coming to get me and now it's midnight and we are just getting there. I try to scout out parking spots as Casey drives slowly through the parking lot. Guess who I see? Lynn is standing outside of her car with her man and his flunkies. Did she think she would be safe because she was with her man?

"Casey, slow down. I'm getting out."

"Aight, you need me?"

"No, I'm good, but if you see someone jumping in, handle your business."

"Aight yo, I got you."

Casey pulls over and I get out of the car. I take the gift I have for Lynn out of the back seat. Casey thought that I was crazier than her for the shit I'm gonna do. I knew that I would see Lynn. I had replayed in my mind a hundred times what I was gonna do to her if I saw her.

She sees me walking toward her, but she acts like she's not worried because I'm alone and she isn't. I walk right up to her with my gift bag in hand and say, "What up?" to her man and his crew. He asks what I have in the bag. I tell him it's something that I need to give to Lynn.

I pull out a big porno-sized battery-operated dildo. Everyone is shocked, including Lynn. They all look like they are confused. Lynn's mouth is wide open. I smile and then smack the shit out of her with the dildo. She is so stunned! I'm able to get a couple of more hits in before she starts fighting back.

Her boyfriend doesn't do anything. He watches us just go at it. She tries to pull a patch out of my hair. I punch her in the eye. She punches me right in my gut and it takes the air out of me. She gets a few more hits in while I'm still hurting from the gut punch. Then I punch her dead in her mouth. I knock out a tooth. *The fellas won't be salivating no more bitch.* I beat her down with a dick because she messed with my old dick. You just don't do that.

The fight goes on for a good three minutes or so. The parking lot security breaks it up and then the police come. We are both arrested. I've been arrested before, but I was bailed out the same day. This time is a different story. It's a Friday night. I won't go before a judge for a bail hearing until Monday. The messed up part is that Lynn would be the person I'd call to get bailed out.

There is no sense in calling Richard because he is out of state. I wouldn't expect him to fly home to bail me out. I will just have to wait this one out. This is not the way I planned on spending my weekend. Crazy Casey didn't even see me get arrested. She didn't wait to see how things played out. She left me and went inside the club once she dropped me off. I know that she won't bail me out. I'm not sure who I am gonna call on Monday. It definitely won't be my mother.

I stay in the same clothes for three days. By the time Monday gets here, I look like a crackhead hoe. I'm still in my club gear. My hair is tore up. I washed my make up off somewhat, but without makeup remover, I couldn't get it all off. My armpits are kicking and my coochie is too. You know you stink when you can smell yourself. I tried to give myself bird baths, but when

47

you got the same panties on for three days it defeats the purpose. I am also getting kind of itchy down there. This bitch was not worth all this suffering.

It's Monday. We have our bail hearing. We are both given the same thousand dollar bail. Her boyfriend comes and picks her up an hour after our hearing. I have no one to call. I racked my brain the entire weekend. There really is no one that I can call except Richard. He won't be home for another five days. Honestly, I don't even know his phone number by heart. These cellphones make you lazy with not having to remember numbers. When I want Richard, I press R and he comes up. I come to grips with the idea that I am going to have to stay in jail until he gets home. This means I will have to go to County until he gets me out on my next court date in three weeks. At least I will get to change my clothes and wash my ass in County.

I thought for sure that Richard would have gotten me out the same night he got home. He didn't come and get me until Tuesday. He was expected to come home on Friday. I'm not sure what took him so long. I knew word had gotten to my mom that I was in here. All he had to do was call her to see where I was at. Right now, I don't even care what his reason is. I'm just happy to be out of there.

He doesn't even speak to me on the drive home. I don't care, because I really don't want to talk about it. While I was beating Lynn's ass, I didn't think about the possibility of getting arrested. My focus was on teaching her ass a lesson. She was talking too much shit and feeling herself way too much to let her slide.

When we get to Richard's crib, I go straight to the bathroom to take a long, hot shower. It feels good to be out. I am not cut out for the correctional-facility life. I need my liberties.

After my shower, I dry off, lotion up and walk out of the bathroom naked. Damn near two weeks has gone by since I had some. I'm ready to fuck. I'm not trying to make love or have sex. I need some of that put-it-down-and-shut-it-down dick from Richard.

Do you know this man still isn't talking to me! He is reading some book on the bed ignoring me. I try to rub up on him and he isn't having it. I'm not used to getting rejected by Richard. This is new for us. I take the hint. I go over to his porn stash, put one in the DVD player and make sure that I put the volume up loud. Then I watch porn right beside him and masturbate until I climax. I do that for one reason: I want to let him know that if he doesn't give it to me, I will still get my shit off without him and I'm bold enough to do it in front of him. I can't stand it when a dude holds out.

I can see that his dick is hard through his shorts. I am down for another round with a willing participant if he would stop being so stubborn. I try one last time to see if he will bite. He is lying down, so I turn over and straddle him. I grind on him with his shorts on. I then lean forward and let my boobs rub against his lips. If this shit doesn't work, I'll have to give it to him, he has some strong willpower.

Next thing you know he's sucking on my titties like his life depends on it. His shorts are down and I'm riding that dick like I ain't had none in two months, never mind two weeks. By the look on his face, I can tell he's beyond pleased. I can also tell he's about to nut. Usually, I wouldn't let him come so quickly, but since I already got mine, I let him get his.

After that episode, things were back to normal. We didn't talk about why I was in jail. He didn't bring it up and neither did I. I was a little embarrassed, but I felt justified. Word on the

49

street was that Lynn was going to bust my ass. If she didn't do it the first time, what makes her

think that she will be able to do it if given another opportunity? She's just mad that I punched

her front tooth out.

Ben:

My secret weapon is being released from prison today. I knew he would accept the job

that I had for him because he had no money and no friends upon his release. I put him up at

one of my properties and said he could live there for three months. He should have completed

his assignment in three months and have enough money to get his own place.

I have one of my assistants pick him up and bring him to his new place. I told him that

I'd meet up with him tonight at the strip club. I'd have a driver pick him up and bring him to the

strip club in Rhode Island. I don't need anyone seeing us together in MA.

I get to the strip club thirty minutes before he's expected to be here. I get a quick lap

dance and have two glasses of Hennessey before he gets here. When he walks in he looks out

of place. He's looking around, obviously looking for me. I tell one of the hostesses to show him

to my table.

He sits down at the table like he's relieved to see someone that he knows. I order him a drink. He got that I'm-wearing-a-wire nervousness with him. He needs to settle the fuck down. I already see this dude can't focus with all this pussy around. I tell two of the strippers that I know who like to make extra-curricular money to go hit him off. I tell them not to get too nasty. I don't know his HIV status. I recommend that they take precautions and to just do enough to get him to nut. They direct me to the Madame of this establishment, who is the owner of the club. I give her two thousand dollars for both of them. I tell her that I want him back here in thirty minutes.

When he comes back, all that nervous energy is gone. He is calm and relaxed. He appears to be more focused. If I go three days without sex, I lose it. I can't imagine going twenty years. I might have to hire those two to hit him off once a week just so that he doesn't rape someone. He is a crazy-ass dude. When I say crazy, I don't mean crazy like shooting someone. I mean white folks crazy, need-to-be-locked-up-in-a-mental-health-facility crazy, kill-your-family-and-yourself crazy.

I go over the plan that I have and he says that he can handle it. If all goes as planned, Craig is going to finally feel my wrath. I got a big stick and I hit hard! I waited twenty years to do this. His payback is almost here.

I leave John here at the club and tell him that the driver will take him back to Boston. I got a couple of more things that I need to get in order. I want this plan to be a success. As I leave the club, I have a smile on my face. Payback is a motherfucker, Craig!

Craig:

The wedding was just like every other wedding that I have been to over the past year with Cynthia. She thought it was beautiful. She liked everything about it. It was a little too bougie for me. You expect folks to cut up on the dance floor at these things. People were acting too sophisticated and shit to even dance. Everyone was two-stepping. If I closed my eyes, I wouldn't have known that these were black people.

As expected, Cynthia thought that I was going to be with her for the rest of the night. As expected, she's pissed when I tell her that's not how it's going down tonight. I have business to take care of. Ava said that she wanted my help purchasing surveillance equipment. I told her that I would meet with her tomorrow. The business that I have to take care of tonight can't wait. I have a jeweler to meet with.

That's right! Your boy is going to propose to Cynthia. I'd be a fool not to. We make a good team. I haven't been able to trust a female, other than Ava and Evelyn, when she was alive. I trust Cynthia with my secrets. If I can do that, she is most definitely going to be my wife.

She sends me a text letting me know that she is disappointed that I didn't spend the remainder of the evening with her. I text her back and tell her that I'm sorry and I will make it up to her. She texts me again and says that I better make it up with a happy face at the end. That's what I like about her, she doesn't like to argue. That could have easily been an argument.

On my way to meet with my jeweler, I hit a lot of traffic. It's that kind of traffic that you might as well roll up a blunt and smoke because you are going to be there for a while. As I roll one up, my phone rings. I connect my phone to the Bluetooth in my car. I need to finish rolling up; my hands need to be free.

I spend an hour with my jeweler. I picked out the stone for Cynthia's engagement ring. This diamond is the size of a nickel. It's flawless and it cost me a lot of money. I will be back to pick it up in a week. Now, I just need to think about how I'm going to propose to her. I can't say that I ever saw myself getting married. So, I have no idea how, where or when I'm going to propose to her. I want it to be special, but at the same time, I want it to be private.

I get a text from Ava. It says that she has reached out to three of my girls and they all accepted her proposition to be part of her private investigating agency. As soon as Ava told me that she was going to reach out to my girls, I immediately started recruiting some other girls to add to my roster. If they weren't going to be as available, then I needed to make sure that I had some girls on deck to fill their spots.

As I'm driving down I-93, I text Ava back. As soon as I hit send, I look up and I'm about to crash into a broken-down car in the motherfucking fast lane. His hazards are on, but I was too busy texting to see that in time. Who expects there to be a stalled-out car in the fast lane? What are the chances of that? I quickly swerve into the middle lane and almost hit a car in the process. Damn! I am lucky. I could have killed myself and the driver at the speed I was going. I gotta stop texting and driving. It's hard though. I always got a lot going on. As soon as I hear that beep, it's hard to ignore it. That beep ain't worth my life. I gotta connect my phone to the car so that my messages are read to me. When I get into the city, I wait until I get to a red light

and text Ava back. My message reads: YOUR BOY ALMOST KILLED HIMSELF TRYING TO REPLY TO YOUR

TEXT. SMH.

Still Bitter Private Investigating Agency

Eve:

I ran into Lynn a couple times and she didn't speak and neither did I. I guess she

changed her mind about busting my ass. I signed up for a GED class. I didn't tell Richard or

anyone else. This is something I want to accomplish for myself. I am tired of working at Wal-

Mart. I am tired of living with Gina. I am old enough to have my own place to stay and a better

source of income. I made many excuses in the past, but I am the only thing getting in the way of

me having a better life.

Since Lynn and I are no longer friends, I have some extra time on my hands to study and

prepare for my test. I took a few tests to see where I ranked grade wise. Come to find out that I

just need to study a few areas and they would let me take the test without going to their pre-

GED exam courses. I guess I am smarter than I gave myself credit.

Studying at home while Gina is here doesn't work. She is too loud and I need peace and quiet. I got myself a library card and started studying there. I like the library. I like to see the books that other people are interested in. I like to people watch and I like the peace that it provides.

At the library, I feel like I have the potential to do anything. After I study, I stay there longer and read all sorts of different books. I like the autobiographies, biographies and fiction by black authors. My favorite book so far is Assata, by Assata Shakur. She is a strong woman living in political exile. I didn't know what political exile was until I read about her. I'm getting much more education teaching myself at the library than I ever did at school.

After I leave the library, I decide to go to Richard's place. He's just getting home from work and he's working on a business plan for his dream of having his own security company. His family has money. He doesn't even have to work if he doesn't want to. He is too proud to live off of his family's money. Richard wants to become a success because of his hard work, not his dad's hard work. His family lives in Massachusetts. He mentioned that he is having a family reunion and his attendance is non-negotiable.

He asks me if I want to go. At first, I am reluctant, but I tell him that I will be happy to go. In the meantime, I gotta handle my business. The reunion is a month away. I will have hopefully passed my GED by then and have another job prospect. I've already applied to a few that required a GED or high school diploma. I figured, by the time I get an interview, I would have passed the exam. I'm keeping my fingers crossed.

I've never been to Massachusetts and honestly never had the desire to go. I mean are there any black people out there? I know that there are some because New Edition and Benzino came from there, but as a whole, I don't think there are many of us out there. In Charlotte, there are a lot of black people. I can't imagine not seeing people that look like me on a daily basis. I tell this to Richard and he says, "You get used to it."

I'm rushing because I am running late to work. Although, I can't stand my job, I need it right now. None of the jobs that I have applied to call me for an interview. I am definitely feeling a little discouraged but I still have some hope. On my lunch break, I'm going to apply to some more jobs. This Wal-Mart shit is for the birds!

Its lunch time and I am on the company computer looking for jobs. I know that's a little scandalous, but the data on my phone plan is almost maxed out for the month. I don't have any extra money to pay for overages. I'm on all the sites applying for everything. On a whim, I even apply for a job in Massachusetts. I have no plans of living out there, but the job seems interesting. I wonder if I'll even get a call back.

On my way home from work, I stop at my favorite soul food spot, Nana's, to get some macaroni and cheese, candied yams and chicken to go. The place is packed as usual. I just want to go home and eat, then relax. The person in front of me can't make up her damn mind. She asks a gazillion questions about how the food is prepared and then takes forever to pay once she gets to the cashier.

It's always when you are in a rush, don't want to be bothered and are tired that shit like this happens. I finally make it out of Nana's without going off on anybody. I get home and Gina is just starting her day at ten o'clock at night. She is turned up to say the least. I can tell she has

had a few already. My attitude goes from funky to funkier when she asks me for money. We

both work at the same place and get the same pay. Where the hell is her money?

I go in my room and shut the door, but not before giving her fifty bucks. She can be so

shady at times. I've asked myself a million times how could this person be my mother. She's

more like a distant relative. She treats me just like any other bitch off of the street. She makes

me feel like she is doing me a favor by allowing me to live with her. I've been trying to stack

lately. I've been putting money aside. I am definitely going to move out. When I do, it will be

abrupt. Gina won't know what hit her.

I should be ready to move out by the time I come back from Massachusetts with

Richard. I've been looking into a few studios and I can afford them even on my Wal-Mart pay. I

want to be able to afford my rent and eat and still have some small luxuries. I can't do that on

Wal-Mart pay. So I am officially on my grind.

I haven't shared any of this with Richard. I want to have everything in place first. I also

know that things can change. I don't want to talk something up and then it doesn't work out. I

rather tell him about it after it's a done deal. So, I will continue to apply to jobs, work extra

shifts at Wal-Mart and prepare for my GED exam.

I was nervous as hell, but I passed! The messed up thing about it is that I had no one to

call. Since I didn't tell anyone that I was preparing for it, I had nobody to celebrate it with. I

guess I could have called Richard, but I don't want him to know that I didn't finish school. That conversation never came up and I didn't offer any information. I think he just naturally assumed that I finished.

So, I celebrated by grabbing a slice of pizza, sneaking it into the library and applying for more jobs. I check my email while I am here. I have an email from a new company that is offering entry level positions. They ask that I answer a few questions and submit it back to them via email. I thought that the few questions were going to be simple.

I'd become accustomed to answering application psychological questions. They basically want to know if you will steal, have you stolen something before and have you been locked up. This questionnaire is very different from anything that I have ever filled out for a job. Answering these questions may take me longer than I expected. There are only three questions. They are like essay questions though. The incident with my ex-boyfriend is still fresh in my mind. So I use that experience to answer the questions:

1. Could you tell if your man was cheating on you? If so, how?
2. Have you ever cheated? If so, why?
3. Did you get back at him for cheating? If so, how? If not, why not?

After I am done, I proofread my answers and hit submit. When I leave the library, I am in a funky mood because I relived the trauma again. I need some dick. Richard should be home soon. I decide to go to his place and wait for him to get home. Once I get here, I figure I'd do some snooping around. I'm not worried about him cheating, but then again, I wasn't worried about my ex either. And I'm not trying to be a victim to that again.

I go through his mail. I go through his medicine cabinet. I go through his dirty laundry. I lift the mattress to see if anything is under it. I was going to go on his laptop, but I don't know his password and don't want to get caught trying to figure it out when he walks through the door. Two minutes later, he walks through the door.

"Did you tell me that you were coming over tonight?

"No, but I didn't think that I had to tell you that I was coming over." I instantly get an attitude.

"Damn, why are you tripping? All I asked is if you told me you were coming over. I thought I may have forgotten. What's up with this attitude? Never mind, I don't even wanna know. I'm gonna put that attitude in check. I'm about to take a shower. When I get out, your ass better be on the bed naked and wet from masturbating. Because, when I get out, I'm gonna eat that pussy up and then beat it up just the way you like it."

My attitude adjusts right on the spot. He knows I like it when he talks to me like that. I don't need any time to masturbate. I was wet as soon as he talked about eating me. That man eats my pussy like it's the best dish he's ever had. He has a nerve to talk shit while he's down there eating it. That just turns me on even more. One of my favorite things he does to me is slowly finger fuck me while he's licking and lightly sucking on my clit. I go crazy when he does that shit! I instantly NEED the dick. This man has me craving his dick. If he cheats, I'm cutting his shit off because nobody else is getting that good dick. Just kidding . . . kinda sorta!

The next morning, I'm sore and a little swollen down there, but I'm good. Today is my day off and I have nothing planned. Richard left for work without waking me up to say bye. I'm grateful for that because I don't like getting woken up for dumb shit. He can tell me good morning when I wake up and call him. I decide to catch up on some reality shows on demand. Then I mentally make plans to go back to the library to apply for more jobs.

When I get to the library, I check my email. To my surprise, there is an email from the job that I had to answer the infamous three questions about cheating. I have a huge grin on my face after I read the email. They want me to come to Massachusetts and interview in person. They said that I could pick between a few dates. Luckily for me, one of those dates coincides with the dates I will be out there for Richard's family reunion.

I never really considered this job seriously. I just wanted to see if I they'd be interested in me. Apparently, they are. I start doing some research about the company. This is a brand new company. There isn't anything on the internet about it. They have a site, but besides that there isn't much information about the company available. Still Bitter Private Investigation Agency would definitely be a gamble if they hired me.

Ava:

Craig was onboard and gave me his blessing to recruit some of his girls. The website was up and running. There were multiple applicants. For the next three weeks, I had interviews set up. I was conducting all of the interviews. Craig said that he would sit in on a few to help out.

I didn't need to interview the three girls that I recruited from Craig. They've worked for Craig for years. I'd been scouting them since I decided to actually make this company a reality. I basically had a meeting with all three of them. I told them my vision. I told them how I thought that they would be an asset to the agency. Then I asked if they were onboard. They all said yes.

All three of them had the skill-set that I needed. They were going to be the team leaders for everyone that I hired through the standard interview process. I could trust those women to handle business for me. I originally thought that I would only use them part time, but the more I thought about it, I knew I needed them full time. Craig wasn't going to be happy, but he'd get over it. I'd just offer him a little more money to soften the blow.

Craig's girls weren't being used to their full potential while they worked for him. I'm nosey as hell and investigating is in my blood. When I say I scouted those females, I'm serious. It was if I was a scout for a basketball team. I went to their games, watched their tapes and reviewed their stats. These bitches were perfect for Still Bitter P.I. Agency.

They have all slept with men for money. I knew that if I needed them to set a dude up, they wouldn't have a problem sleeping with him. I would use them for those times. The new hires, I couldn't trust nor could I expose them to that. The last thing I needed was for one of them to get into some trouble and crack under pressure. So, I will leave the heavy lifting to the team leaders.

My agency is becoming a living, breathing thing. I took all of the necessary steps to make sure my shit was legit. I hired an expensive accountant to make sure my money stays right and no IRS problems develop. Things are looking up.

I still haven't decided on a health insurance package. It, honestly, will be cheaper for me to pay the premiums on individual policies if I have them sign up for the health care exchange. Better yet, just say fuck it and don't offer insurance and pay the penalty. I'm sure it's cheaper than signing up for a commercial group policy. I gotta figure that piece out soon.

I've invested a lot into this agency. I bought the building instead of leasing. The building was part commercial part residential. So, now I'm a landlord. There are twenty units in the building that will house Still Bitter P.I. Agency. My accountant calculated that the rent that I will collect made this purchase a win-win situation.

Starting next week, interviews will be held. I have some stagers from Lynn coming in to decorate my office and the reception area. I was going to go with this agency that was featured in the Best of Boston Home Magazine, but then I heard about these three relatives that were supposedly what I needed in my life.

They are three black women from Lynn that started their own business decorating and staging. They've only been in business for a year, but I'd seen the properties that they've decorated and staged. I was beyond impressed. So, I hired N3 Decorating.

Interviews are almost over. Craig has business to take care of. I am going to do the very last interview without him. I have room for one more person. If I'm not feeling this last one, then I'll have to continue to interview. As I'm reviewing her responses to the questionnaire, she walks in and introduces herself.

I almost shit on myself when I see her face. It's like I am looking at my daughter Karma, except she had dark eyes and blonde weave. My mind must be playing tricks on me. The person that she resembles is dead. Her mom is dead. Her grandparents are dead. Her Uncle Brian and his immediate family are dead. That whole family is dead and gone with the exception of Ben. She can't be who I think she is? It's not possible! I'm tripping.

I don't think I hear one thing that she says during the interview. I just keep looking at her. I keep studying her. Is it her? It can't be. Could it? According to her application, she is from Charlotte, not Boston. When she's done talking, I tell her that I will get back to her tomorrow with the date and time for the second interview. I let her know that it will be a group interview and it will take place this week.

Craig calls me and asks how the last interview went. I tell him that it went well and that I am probably going to hire her. He asks if she is a dime or does she need a makeover. I tell him that she is beautiful and would be a great addition to the team. He doesn't ask what her qualifications are or anything. All he wants to know is what she looks like. I should have said she looked like Charlene's daughter, but I didn't. I need to do some more investigating before I let him in on my suspicions.

As I am driving home, I can't stop thinking about the possibility of Eve from Charlotte being Evelyn from Boston. I still have the baby picture that Charlene sent me via email. When I get home, I head to the computer to pull up that picture. I then log into my system at work and pull up the video footage. I taped each interview. Eve is definitely baby Evelyn all grown up.

63

It is group interview day. Today is Karma's first day working as my receptionist. I wanted to see her reaction when Eve walks in. They have different styles of dress. Their hairstyles are different, but they resemble each other so much. My office has a two way mirror. I can see what's going on in the reception area but they can't see inside my office.

Karma's on the phone when Eve walks in. Eve has on a navy blue pencil skirt with a lavender-flowery blouse. She doesn't have on stilettos like most of the other girls. She has on nude-kitten heels. Her outfit actually reminds me of her namesake. Evelyn dressed like this when she was alive. All that she was missing was the pearls. I get a lump in my throat because Evelyn's death still hurts me.

Eve waits patiently for Karma to acknowledge her. Karma doesn't look at Eve, she doesn't even look at her to mouth the words "one moment." Although Eve is dressed sophisticated like my late friend Evelyn, my gut tells me she is not what she seems. I bet she is more like me when I was that age. This means, if Karma doesn't acknowledge her soon, shits about to go down.

Eve walks up closer to the desk where Karma is talking on the phone. She puts her bag down on the desk and it knocks over Karma's bottle of water. Karma jumps up in an attempt to avoid the spill on her outfit, but she wasn't quick enough. Eve apologizes like she is so sorry. Karma's first instinct usually is to go off! She can't help it. It's in her blood. She doesn't do it though. She plays it off like it isn't a big deal. She then asks Eve her name and tells her to have a seat. Group interviews are being held in fifteen minutes.

After the interviews were completed, I meet with each person individually to tell them if they will be becoming a part of our team. When I get to Eve, I tell her that I like her style. She asks what I mean by that. I tell her that I watched the entire scene from my office. I knew that she purposefully spilled the water on the receptionist.

Eve starts to apologize and explain. I hold my hand up and tell her that there is no need to go on. Eve asks if that is why she isn't going to be hired to work for the agency. I tell her that that is the reason why she IS going to be hired. She got Karma's ass off of the phone. Karma ultimately gave Eve the courtesy she deserves. She acknowledged her.

Eve looks shocked that she actually got the job. I tell her that I want the new hires to start in three weeks. I tell her the pay and that she will have an additional fifteen hundred dollars included in her first check as a sign-on offer. She says that she definitely accepts the position and will see me in three weeks ready to work.

When she walks out of the office, she goes straight to Karma's desk and apologizes again. She also told Karma that she hopes that little mishap doesn't ruin the chance for them to become friends, since they will be working together. All I can do is laugh. I know Karma isn't feeling her, but Eve is killing her with passive-aggressive kindness. Eve is going to fit right in just fine.

I email all of the new hires their packet. It includes the agency expectations, their specific pay, the job description, their schedule and their new corporate American Express account. The group that I pick is definitely a mixed group. They come from all walks of life. I can

65

see some of them clashing, but they are going to have to work past that. This is a good job and if they want to keep it, they will act like they know better.

Karma:

I hat bitch thought that she was cute. I knew she spilled that water on me on purpose. She said that she was sorry, but I knew that she was fronting. I can't stand bitches. She couldn't just wait until I got off of the phone. It's not like she was late. She was early. If common sense was applied she would have sat her ass down like everyone else did.

This chick had the nerve to come back out and rub it in my face that she got the job. She acted like her intent was to apologize but again, I knew that she was fronting. She wasn't sorry for spilling water on me. She was gloating in her own way. This shit wasn't over. If she was going to be working here she was going to have to straighten the fuck up and act right. She had no idea who she was messing with. I may look sweet, cute and friendly, but I am Ava's daughter after all.

I can't wait to get out of here and go to the gym. I know Ray is going to be there. He is going to ask me out tonight. He doesn't know it yet, but he will. I've already planned it out. Now I just need to go home and get one of my sexy workout outfits. I pick out a blood-red number. I figure it's appropriate because I am going for the kill.

My new trainer and now friend, Lamont, is onboard with my plan to make Ray my man. I get to the gym and immediately start working out with Lamont. After about twenty minutes, I fake an injury. Lamont makes a big deal about it. So big of a deal that Ray comes out to see what is up. Lamont insists that I need to be taken to a hospital. I tell Ray that I am ok and don't need any medical attention. That's what I tell him, but that's not how I act.

Ultimately, we decide that it's best for Ray to take me home, if I am comfortable with it. He tells me that if I don't feel better tomorrow, I should go to the hospital and that he will pay for the services. Since I am limping, he helps me all the way into my place. Thank God my mom is out.

Since he brings me all the way into my home, I know he is feeling me. He makes sure that I don't need anything. He wants everything to be within reach so that I don't have to put too much pressure on my leg. I knew that I just needed to get him outside of his work environment in order to get his undivided attention. I usually don't have to work this hard, but Ray is a different type of creature. At the end of the day, he is still a man.

By the time he left, we have a date planned for when my injury heals. We decide on a date two weeks from now. I am so excited, but I will not show it. I don't want to gas him up so soon. He's fine as hell, so I know he is used to the attention. I'm even finer, so he won't catch me openly sweating him. He needs to feel like he just hit the Mega Millions getting a date with me. So, when the two weeks come up, I will not be available.

I will make sure that we talk frequently between now and then. Make sure I give him something to crave and then when it's time to meet, cancel on him. I need to be in control of this relationship. Lord knows that I don't really want to cancel, but this is the game I will have to play.

This man is good looking and has deep pockets. If I'm going to lock him down, I can't show him how bad I want him. I really have to be pleasant to him, but nonchalant at the same time. This shit is a serious intricate game. It will take exceptional skills to have this man eating out of the palm of my hand or eating something else. Let the games begin.

Eve:

I can't believe this! I actually got the job. It's a damn good job at that. As soon as I get back to Charlotte I am giving my notice. Now, I just need to figure out where I am going to live. Since I am here, I figure it would be wise to start looking at apartment listings. A nice one bedroom apartment in Boston would be ideal. Once I see how much they cost, I know that I won't be living in Boston.

Boston is expensive! I have no problem living outside of the city and commuting in, especially if it saves me hundreds of dollars. I have to tell Richard this stuff today. I don't know how he is going to take it. I almost don't want to say anything until after we get back to Charlotte. In the meantime, I'm going to start looking into studio apartments.

I haven't met his family yet. He decides that I will get to meet everyone at the family reunion banquet tonight. The theme is red and black. As much as I want to wear red, I feel that it will be more appropriate for me to wear black. I want to leave a good impression. Whenever I put on red, I'm looking for attention and I'm sure to get it. I look good in red. My body looks good in just about anything and any color. So, black will do.

After my group interview, I go shopping. Richard takes me to the Cambridge Side Galleria Mall. He tells me that he will treat me to an outfit for the banquet tonight. I start to walk straight into bebe, but then I change my mind and walk right past it into Ann Taylor. I need something that doesn't look like I was going to the club.

Don't get me wrong, I have classy conservative clothes, but not my dresses. All of the dresses I have are for the club. I never went anywhere nice. Therefore, there was no need to go to buy a nice going out dress. Today was just a great day. I felt like Julia Roberts going out dress shopping with Richard Gear, except I wasn't a hoe.

I try on about five dresses and can't decide between two of them. So, he buys both of them for me. I am so appreciative and grateful. I really didn't expect him to buy me two dresses. When I asked him which one he wants me to wear, he tells me to surprise him. He is definitely getting some pussy tonight.

When we get back to the hotel, he orders me to bend over on the bed. I guess he is getting his pussy right now and isn't waiting until tonight. And I am ok with this. I have on a skirt. So all he has to do is pull my panties down and give me that dick. I swear. I daydream about his chocolate dick. It's the perfect length, the perfect width and has the perfect curve. We ain't breaking up. I can't see myself without his dick. He's gonna have to move to Boston with me.

As we are lying in bed, I tell him that I have some good news. Before he can ask what the good news is, his phone rings. It's his mother. I can't hear what she is saying, but I can hear his responses.

"Yes Mom, she's with me. No, she's not bringing any of her kids. Mom, I told you that she doesn't have kids. Don't worry! She won't be dressed like a floozy. I miss you too, and I will see you tonight, Mom. Bye."

"I can't *wait* to meet your mom." I say sarcastically.

"Don't trip. I told you how she is. Don't take any of it to heart. She just wants her sons to have good women by their side. You are definitely a good woman. You are sweet, loyal, sexy, smart and have a nice weave."

I look at him like he's crazy and swing my weave playfully in his face. We both end up cracking up. I never got a chance to tell him my good news. I guess we will talk about it tonight. I didn't know that he thought that I was smart. I knew he thought that I was fine, but not smart. That just makes me love him more. Damn, did I just say love?

Craig:

Ava texts me. She says that she wants to take me to dinner to celebrate. She is now fully staffed. She already has clients lined up for her services. I thought that she would have had to work hard to get people to pay her to find out fucked-up shit about their lover. Ava linked up with an elite marketing firm and had clientele lined up in a matter of two weeks.

These people are paying good money for her services. I may need to look into partnering up with Ava instead of getting a stipend. We are gonna have to talk about this some more. I need to consolidate my various businesses. I am getting older. I need to do less ripping and running around. I am making good money, but I definitely need to look into doing something with a little less risk.

I'm going to marry Cynthia. I definitely need to slow down a bit. Cynthia's only complaint is that I don't spend enough time with her. She feels like my attention is always divided. I can't front. It is always divided. Even my sleep is affected by my racing mind. My sleep is always interrupted. I'm always thinking about my next move and the three moves that will follow it.

I can't help it. How else am I gonna stay on point and on top? I've been building my empire since back in the day. I'm finally comfortable with the level of wealth I've acquired. Yeah, ya boy just said "acquired." When you deal with people that make "fuck you money" you gotta strengthen that vocab. I'm finally at a point to where I'm making "fuck you money" too. You got power when you got "fuck you money." That's when you don't NEED for anything and anything you WANT you can buy. You can be an asshole. You've earned that right. Most motherfuckers with a shitload of money are assholes. You almost have to be one to make any real money.

Cynthia has no idea that I'm proposing to her. It's going down this weekend. I'm taking her to Foxwoods in Connecticut to see her "boyfriend" John Legend. We will be spending the night there. When we make it back to our room after the concert, she will have the surprise of her life. I can't imagine that she would ever picture her proposal going down like this. "Fuck you money" made what's about to go down possible.

She loves her "boyfriend." That's all she kept talking about after the concert. She told me that I'm lucky he's taken because she would have given him the panties. Every now and then she says things that I don't expect from her. She's usually reserved, but every once and a while the not so conservative Cynthia reveals herself. The more I think about it, the more she reminds me of Evelyn. She looks nothing like her, but she carries herself like her.

Nobody knows it, but Evelyn's death ripped me to shreds. I actually cried. I say actually, because I hardly ever cry. People come and go a lot in the game. Funerals come with the territory, but when baby girl got killed, I was all in my feelings. If I ever loved a female it was her. I know she was with that dude Fritz for a while and even married him, but he wasn't right for her. That's why she was so on the fence about him. Had I been more straight-laced, I know she would have been my lady. I just couldn't get out of that life. Here I am twenty years later, finally considering getting out of the game. Finally ready to settle down.

We walk down the hotel corridor and she can hear one of John Legend's songs playing. She looks at me and asks if I left the radio on or programmed it so it would be on when we arrived. I just smile at her. She opens the hotel door and the room is decorated with red and white roses. Roses were everywhere. We have a suite that is like our own apartment. There is a red carpet that leads from the foyer to the bedroom.

She gives me a what-the-heck-is-going-on-in-here look. She then says, "You left the music on pretty loud, but that system is good. Is it Bose? I'm surprised no one complained about the noise level. You've got that shit turned up like the concert is on our bedroom."

I laugh and say, "Maybe it is."

She opens the door to the bedroom and the music stops long enough for her to actually take in what was going on and then the beat drops and picks back up at the hook.

Baby, tonight's the night I let you know
Baby, tonight's the night we lose control
Baby, tonight you need that, tonight believe that
Tonight I'll be the best you ever had

There is a live band playing. I had the hotel staff remove the bed and put down a dance floor in our room so that she can dance with her "boyfriend" for the first and last time; because after tonight she will be all mine. John Legend dances with my lady while he sings to her. Then, I cut in before the song ends, get down on one knee and present her with an uncut seven-carat diamond. I tell her that she can have it cut and designed in whatever setting that she wants. Then, I ask her to marry me.

She says yes and cries like I've never seen her cry before. John Legend leaves an autographed CD for Cynthia and makes his exit. I get the best head I've ever gotten from

73

Cynthia tonight. I wear that ass out. We make love to John Legend's CD and have it on repeat.

The sex is so good, I wonder if she is imaging that J. Legend is hitting it. The next morning, I

have the jeweler meet me at our suite and let Cynthia design her own ring.

Ben:

John said that he'd been watching her for two weeks. He knows her routine and has her

schedule down to a science. He figured out the perfect time to scoop her up unnoticed. He was

going to do it this morning. He'd be waiting for her at her office.

On Tuesdays, she goes to work early. She is there before any of her co-workers for at

least forty-five minutes to an hour. Today will be a bad day for her. For a fleeting second, I

almost feel bad for her. She is a necessary casualty of a long, drawn-out war. Today will be the

woman's last day on earth. Today Craig will feel like he's amongst the walking dead.

John said he'd call me on my pre-paid minute phone when he's done. The entire

workday is over and I've yet to hear from John. Something must have gone wrong or he is really

crazier than I thought and is still torturing her. When I speak to John, he sounds all nervous and

shit.

"Yo B . . . it's done. I did it."

"Now what exactly did you do?"

"I did what you told me to do man!"

"Who the fuck are you raising your voice at!"

"I'm just saying . . . the job is done. When can I expect the rest of my money?"

"You'll get your motherfucking money once I get the confirmation I need."

"You obviously haven't seen the news, turn it on and hit me up when you get your confirmation. I need all of my money man. Shit's hot right now for me. This is not a time for me to be low on funds."

Click. I hang up the phone and turn on the news. How did I miss this? On every news station the heading reads: BREAKING NEWS.

"Cynthia Brooks was found by fellow employees in the Swampscott Real Estate office this morning with a gunshot wound to the head. Officials say that luckily someone came into work early that morning and found her. Paramedics tried to stabilize her and got her to nearby Salem Hospital. Cynthia is listed in critical condition and is in a coma. A few witnesses say that a black man about six feet tall and in his fifties was acting suspicious while walking around in this Swampscott neighborhood this morning. They had never seen him before, but didn't want to make too big of a deal out of it due to the sensitivity that surrounded the Trayvon Martin case years ago. Rick back to you."

This crazy-ass dude really did it. She wasn't pronounced dead, but I'm sure she won't survive a bullet to the head. He used a silencer, so nobody heard the bullet, but he didn't make sure that he wasn't seen hanging around in the neighborhood. His black ass might be headed

75

right back to jail. And he better keep his mouth shut. It's not my fault that his dumb ass made himself visible to the public.

Enough with that, I need to put my ear to the streets and see what Craig's people are talking about. From what I can gather, nobody knows anything about my involvement, which is how I want to keep it. If I know Craig, he won't rest until he finds out who tried to shoot his new fiancé. I need to get John out of the area ASAP.

I withdraw the money from my account and buy him a ticket to San Francisco, CA. Nobody will look for him there. Cali has so many homeless people roaming the streets that John will blend right in. He has a homeless look about him. I lease an apartment for him and pay for the year upfront. This dude has no reason to be homeless and he has a year of free rent. I also hit him off with thirty thousand dollars. I tell him to lose my number and forget that he ever knew me. He tells me to do the same.

I know Craig has to be trying his best to figure out who would try to kill his girl and not him. I want him to go crazy trying to find out. I also want him to hurt the way that I did when he killed my wife and daughter. He didn't stop there. He killed my brother and his family too. He had no conscience back then. I'm not sure if he's grown one now, but I've lost mine all together.

I want that piece of shit to cry like I did for months on end. I want him to beat himself up for living the lifestyle that he leads. I want him to blame himself for his fiancé's death. He needs to suffer like I have. I want him to lose faith in love, lose faith in humanity. Motherfucker just lose faith! I want him to want to die. I knew that he would find someone that he loved eventually. So I waited patiently. Now he will know what it feels like to lose the love of his life. I replay in my mind that period of my life.

Since Ava and I were no longer seeing each other, I had to get my head from somewhere else. I stayed out the night before. I'd had sex with two hoes and they still couldn't satisfy me the way Ava did. Once I got tired or them, I went home to my wife.

I expected her to have an attitude because I stayed out all night. I didn't call or text. I just stayed out. I'm not sure if she was used to it or reached a point where she just didn't give a fuck. Either way, I felt a little uneasy when I walked through the door.

It was seven a.m. Charlene wasn't home and it didn't look like she had slept there either. My first instinct was to think that she was cheating on me. Then, I thought about it with a clearer mind. She wasn't cheating on me. She probably spent the night out at a relative's house or something. She could have at least texted me or left me a note.

Charlene never came back. I called myself staying in to chill that day; give the streets a break. It wasn't until one of my associates came over and said that I had a serious problem and that I may need to relocate for a minute. I wasn't relocating for anybody! I wanted to know what had this dude so spooked.

By the time he finished updating me on what was going on in the streets while I was out chasing pussy, I was numb. I went through all the stages of grieving in a matter of ten seconds. I chose to remain at the angry stage. I was never able to leave that stage. I'm still there, but hopefully this payback that I put on Craig will finally give me some peace. I became real bitter after losing all of my family. Every time I see Craig or his people all I can think about is revenge. He crossed the line. I didn't kill anyone in his family. So what I fucked up Ava's face. She lived. He killed my wife and anyone else that ever mattered to me. For that he is going to pay. And that's exactly what is transpiring now. It is time for Craig to pay.

The plan actually worked out better than I planned. The fact that she isn't technically dead and in a coma will mess with Craig's head even more than if she had died on the spot. Her dying would hurt him, but at least it is final and he could deal with it and find some closure. Cynthia isn't dead though. She is in a coma. I doubt she will live and if she does, she'll probably have the brain of a two-year old. What I'm happy about is that he will be suffering and stressing over the unknown. Will she live? If she lives will she be a vegetable? Will their lives ever be the same? Will they ever get married? I want him to die from the unknown; not knowing if she will recover and not knowing who did this to her.

Ava:

Oh My God! I can't believe this shit. The police just have a lame-ass description of some middle-aged-black guy walking the streets. They got that description from white people. That could be anybody! I am going to conduct my own investigation. I have a feeling because Cynthia is Craig's girlfriend, they aren't going to be extremely motivated to solve the case.

The police hate Craig. They stay trying to put him in prison. Craig keeps his hands clean

for the most part. So, they've had a hard time sticking something on him. I feel like this is their

way of getting back at him and not having to do the dirty work. I know Craig isn't going to rely

on the police to solve this. I'm betting that Craig hopes they never find the guy who did this. He

is going to want to handle this himself. Kind of like when he handled things for me with Ben

twenty years ago.

When Craig hits, he hits hard! It's like he turns off whatever compassion he has and

becomes an animal. He got rid of everyone in Ben's family because Ben threw battery acid in

my face. He says that *I'm* a little extreme. He says that *I* overreact. I got nothing on Craig in the

overreacting department. If you step on his shoe, he wants to cut your foot off so that it will

never happen again. If you step on my shoe, I'm stepping right back on your shoes with my

highest heels on and with more aggression.

Tonight I really just need to unwind. I go check in on Cynthia but don't stay long. She

already looks like she is dead. She looks lifeless. She is unresponsive. Craig's sitting beside her.

He looks like he hasn't slept in a week. He keeps pacing the floor and talking to himself out

loud. If she doesn't pull through, I feel bad for whoever has their hand in this. Craig is ready for

war.

I go home and my mother is all in my business. I can't even walk in the door and she's

asking me a million-and-one questions. I know she is genuinely concerned about Cynthia, but

I'm just not in the mood for twenty questions. I tell her to watch the news if she wants an update. As I walk up the stairs, I hear her call me a bitch. I'm gonna let that one slide. I am being

a bitch. I'm not in a good mood and she isn't good at reading people, obviously.

When I finally come back downstairs, my mood is a little better. I guess my mother's

isn't because she tells me that she ran into Rochelle and she asked how I was wearing my hair

nowadays. I stick my middle finger up at my mother. I know she didn't run into Rochelle. She is

just starting shit with me. It's been decades since that day my mother held me down while she

let Rochelle butcher my hair and I'm still bitter. My mother knows that. That's why she said it.

As I sit at the kitchen island, I think about what else is stressing me. I have a lump on my

left breast that is starting to worry me. When I first found it, I searched my right breast

desperately to see if the lump was on that side too. I remember when I was younger the

gynecologist would always remind me to do self-breast exams. The doctor would also say if you

find a lump or a bump on one side make sure that it's on the other side too. If not, make sure I

make an appointment to be examined.

I knew that I needed to make an appointment. I just didn't want to deal with it. I wished

it would just go away on its own. It's been three months. It hasn't gone away on its own. How

do you want an answer, but don't want an answer at the same time? I'm shook. Everything is

always the worst-case scenario with me. That is why I haven't made an appointment.

I mean damn, I already went through ten thousand surgeries to make my face look

halfway normal again. I feel like I've had my fair share of pain. My mom hated me as a child. I

never knew my white father. My husband cheats on me, has me jumped and then has a baby

with the woman he cheated on me with. I lose one of my best friends. Soon after, I lose my

80

other best friend. I get drugged and raped by Ben and then he comes back and splashes battery acid in my face. Breast cancer would confirm that God doesn't know me or love me.

I hate this feeling! It's that feeling when everything good seems to be happening to other people and the bad that is left over is saved for you. It's at these times where I don't know how I am going to make it. Each day is dreaded and I don't know how I can ever feel good again. Each incident that I mentioned in my past made me feel like that. I couldn't see how there could ever possibly be a brighter day. My future seems dark.

The only good thing that I have in my life is my daughter Karma. She came from a bad situation, but turned into such an enormous blessing. My life is nothing like I thought it would be. I never thought I'd have a child out of wedlock. I didn't plan on having a child with my husband's brother. I never could have imagined having a child with my best friend's husband. I never would have thought that I'd no longer have either of my best friends. I really miss Evelyn and Charlene. Thank God for Lance.

Speaking of Lance, he's been in a foul mood. He thinks his husband is cheating on him. He wants me to investigate. He said that he wants to be my first client. I told him that I would never take his money. My loyalty is to him. If he wants me to find out if his husband is cheating, I will do it for free. He's pissed because they are so far along into the adoption process. He wouldn't have agreed to adopt if he was going to be a single parent. His husband better not be cheating on him.

Craig:

Cynthia has been in a coma for days now. I miss her so much. She's here but she's not. I miss her calling me and texting me throughout the day. Even the simple shit like how's my day or that she's thinking about me. You don't realize how much you enjoy those little things until you ain't getting them no more.

One second I'm planning our future and the next I gotta think about if I need to make funeral arrangements. God sure is messing with my head. I don't talk about him too much. I figure he's been good to me. He's kept me out of jail and kept me alive. What more could I ask for? Maybe this is his way of saying don't push it. Maybe that's why Cynthia is in a coma and could die.

I feel powerless. It doesn't matter who I kill. It won't bring Cynthia back to me. Only God can bring her back. I don't want her to be a vegetable either. It's not that I wouldn't take care of her, but I know she wouldn't want to live like that. She'd rather "go on home to glory" as she would say. God, please wake her up and let her be in her right mind when she does.

I haven't left the hospital because I don't want to risk Cynthia waking up and me not being here. The doctors tell me that there is no way to tell when she will come out of the coma or if she will come out of the coma. I'm supposed to just deal with that and go on about my day. Nothing about my day is the same anymore. All this shit feels foreign to me.

I end up leaving to go home and shower. When I walk into the bedroom of our home, I can smell Cynthia. I just want to have her lying beside me telling me about her hectic day. I want to hear her laugh again. When something is really funny to her she snorts. I miss her snorts. I miss her kiss. This woman has the softest lips. Damn, baby, please wake up! I need you!

I try to hold back the tears, but they won't stop. I want to make a sound, but I can't. Nothing will come out, just tears. I cried hard that night. I cried for her and I cried for Evelyn. The tears for Evelyn were long overdue. I got on my knees for the first time in years and pleaded with God to have mercy on Cynthia and wake her up. Lord, I believe in you. The doctors say that she may not be the same. The Lord I know can fix this. Wake her up Lord and bring her back to me. In the meantime, motherfuckers are gonna pay!

The next morning, I have a meeting with my goons. Their assignment is to find out who's trying to get at me through Cynthia. I know that whoever did this to Cynthia is really trying to hurt me. I know the tactic. I've used it myself. Go for the loved ones if you want to hit them hard. The last person I had to handle like that was Ben. That was almost two decades ago. He couldn't possibly be trying to get back at me. If he is, he sure waited a long ass time to do it. I'm going to have to look into that possibility. If he did arrange this, there is nothing that Ava could say to get me to spare him this time around.

Eve:

We get to the banquet and I'm feeling good because I know that I look good. I have on a form fitting black dress that has a low back. There's a black sequin stripe that lines up perfectly with the crack of my ass all the way down to the bottom of the dress. I have my blonde hair pulled back in a sleek ponytail. I have on fake pearl earrings with a matching fake pearl bracelet.

Richard said that I look beautiful. I feel beautiful. That was until I was in the bathroom and overheard two bitches talking about me. I'm not sure if they knew that I was in the bathroom or not. They may have known and didn't care. They were hating on me hard.

"Did you see that hootchie mama dress Richard's date has on?"

"I know! For real! Where did she think that she was going with that dress on?"

"She's cute, but she could use some tips in the wardrobe department."

"I bet she got that outfit from Burlington Coat Factory or something! Where'd he find her, in the projects?"

"Girl you ain't right! Did you see the fake pearl set she has on? It isn't even a good fake set!"

"Well she must be putting it down in the bed because Richard wouldn't give me the time of day! And I openly flirted with him."

"Really, that's not like him. You told me that he is usually down for a quickie when he comes back to Massachusetts. I wonder what's changed."

"The slut must swallow!"

They both left the bathroom laughing. They were some bold-ass bitches if they knew I was in the bathroom stall and was still talking shit. At first, I wanted to cry. After that emotion passed, I wanted to beat their asses. I didn't tell Richard what went down. One of the females was his cousin and the other was her best friend. The rest of the night, I felt funky. I tried my best to be fake and smile the entire night.

I don't remember anyone's name. I didn't even flinch when his mom started giving me shade. She asked questions that basically spelled out how she thought of me.

"Have you thought about furthering your education and going to a community college?"

No Bitch and why did it have to be a community college?

"Where did you say you met my son again . . . at a bar?"

No Bitch, I met him at the club. Next question. I wanted so badly to say this out loud. It was hard as hell not to go off on folks up in there. They made me feel so unwelcomed.

"I met Richard at a night club in Charlotte."

"Yeeeees, yeeeees the bar and you are still holding strong. People that meet in a bar usually only make it a one night affair," she says and laughs in bougie-ass tone.

I am trying my very best not to go off on her, but she is pushing it. She is basically saying that her son is just supposed to hit it and quit it. Well he hit it and can't quit it. That's how good my coochie is, future mother-in-law. This bitch is really testing me. One more snide remark and

I'm leaving. I'm not going to make a scene, because I know that's what she is waiting on. She is

dying for me to give her a reason to call me ghetto.

Craig:

When you live life from one hustle to the next you don't think about slowing down.

Slowing down won't get me paid. Life has always been about making money. Period. I make

plans to slow down and this shit happens.

It makes me question shit. Is this my punishment for living a fast lifestyle? What choice

did I have? It's not like I had a lot of options. Like many black men, I grew up without my dad. I

knew who the motherfucker was. He acted like he didn't know who I was.   My mother

talked so much shit about him to me that I wasn't even messed up about this dude not claiming

me. She talked so much shit that it made me not like him before I got the chance to know him.

Turns out she was right. My dad ain't shit.

I made sure that I met him, though. Moms told me that he left when I was two. I really

had no memory of him. Moms kept tabs on his whereabouts. I never understood why she

would keep tabs on someone that obviously didn't care about her or their son. I think about the

first time that I met him.

Out of the blue, I asked her where this motherfucker lived. To my surprise, she walked

over to her bible and pulled out a piece of paper ripped off from a Marriott notepad. All of his information was on it. I didn't want to think about how she got that piece of paper, but I had a pretty good idea. She definitely was keeping in touch with him on a level I didn't want to even think about.

I took the piece of paper out of her hand and stuffed it into my jeans pocket. I looked at the address and recognized the street. At that moment, I decided it was time to take a walk to meet my father. This fool lived less than two miles away and never bothered to show his face. I was only in the eighth grade by that point, but I felt like he missed my whole life.

As I walked up Blue Hill Ave, I started thinking about all of the things I was going to say to him. I wanted to go off on him and tell him how he missed out on knowing his son. I wanted to tell him all of the things that he was supposed to do with me that he didn't. I wanted to tell him that I needed him. Moms couldn't do it all.

Evelyn Street was full of three family homes lined up on top of each other. Everybody on the street was black. Some of them differentiated themselves from being black. Well, not some of them, just one group, the Haitians. For some reason, they thought that they were better than the regular black folks that lived in the hood. The women had this attitude like they were entitled to shit and like they were better than everyone else. The men were pussies that didn't know how to let go of their mother's titties.

I walked to my dad's porch, I saw three dudes sitting on the steps. One of them was at the top step sitting with his sunglasses on and it's well past daylight hours. They all had on white tees, jeans, wave caps and crisp white Air force Ones.

They were drinking beer and smoking weed. That shit was strong too. I could smell it when I was three houses away. The fool rocking the shades at seven o'clock at night was staring at me. Although, I couldn't see his eyes, I could tell. I walked right up to them and said, "Y'all know where Blue is?"

Simultaneously, the two dudes without the shades stood up with the quickness, pulled out their gats and spat, "Who the fuck wanna know?" as if it were scripted. I had two dudes with their guns pointed at my head acting hard. All I wanted to know was where my dad was. I was so afraid that I almost pissed on myself. I was definitely shook. I know that was the effect that they were looking for.

Mattapan dudes were so over the top with trying to be hard. These same dudes referred to Mattapan as Murderpan. They acted like they were soldiers or something. They needed to chill. I was in junior high school. I couldn't possibly look like a threat, but there they were acting like I was about to take out their shaded leader. I'd figured out the dynamics and deduced that the dude with the shades was the boss.

When I was about to answer the two stooges question, I heard two loud mouth Haitian girls coming out of the shop P&R with coco bread and cheese patties. I was embarrassed because I had guns pointed at me and I know I looked like a punk standing there. The two girls walked right by me as if they didn't see the guns pointed at me and said something in Kreyól. I made a note to remember the word that they called me so I could ask somebody what it meant. It sounded like "mar-cici". I didn't have to know the language to know that they were talking shit. I gave them a fuck you stare, but I'm not sure if they even noticed.

I looked up at the dude in the shades and said, "Blue, you gonna let ya goons point a gun at your son's head?" He took his shades off for all of five seconds and looked me up and down. Then he ordered them to put their guns away. That was how I met my dad.

I started visiting my dad without my Mom's knowledge from that point on every day after school. I thought that my visits would lead to some type of bonding, but that didn't happen. I ended up pumping for him. That is how my career in drug dealing began.

By the ninth grade, I realized that my dad was no good. He was everything that my mom said he was. I was usually punctual, but that day everything was just going wrong. I ended up getting to one of my designated spots really late. As a result, I messed up Blue's money. He found this out and put my shit on blast in front of everyone. He called me all types of fucked-up names. He even had the nerve to call me a "bitch" just like my "bum-ass-bitch mama." He had a loud mouth and everyone on the block heard him go in on me.

I will never forget that day. I can't remember a day where I ever felt more humiliated, embarrassed and small. That was my last day on Evelyn Street. I learned some valuable lessons on that street. What I learned, I took with me. I was my father's apprentice. When that was over, I took the opportunity to work with the dudes that were trying to cut in on my dad's "business."

I actually sought them out. I wanted my father to feel betrayed. It was only right. That's how I felt . . . betrayed. Let him feel what I felt for a while. So, I decided to hit him where it hurt; in his pockets. Once I linked up with the rival crew, I went through the ranks rather quickly. I started selling weed for them at first. Then I stepped it up a few notches. I used the uncanny business mind that I didn't know that I had. I showed them how to make a bigger profit selling the type of drugs that will get you serious time.

I started out doing that to teach my father a lesson and show him that I could play his game and perfect the craft better than him. Little did I know, I'd become so good at it that I'd decide to make a career out of it. By tenth grade, all of the young dudes that worked for my father were now working for me. Except for those two goons that never left his side. I wouldn't have them working for me anyway.

By eleventh grade, he fell off. He stopped dealing in the drug world. He couldn't hang. He was messing with too many bitches. By my senior year, he ended up dying from AIDS. I didn't go to the funeral. My moms went. I didn't want her to go. I told her that he didn't care nothing about her. He talked mad shit about her. She wanted to know how I knew what he said about her. That's when I realized I slipped up. I never told her about the times I spent with him and what I did for him. I never told her that he thought she was a "bum-ass bitch."

Eve:

I'm on American Airlines headed back to Charlotte, NC. Richard is sitting in the aisle seat and I'm in the middle seat. The person in the window seat is an elderly white-haired white lady with way too much flowery perfume on. As soon as she sits down, I get an instant headache. The shit she has on could kill someone.

Not only that but she is extra talkative. *Do I look like I want to talk to you lady?* I can tell that she is going to talk my ear off the entire two-hour flight. Not only does she talk my ear off, but she keeps coughing without covering her mouth. *Now she should know better.* I keep holding my breath every time she coughs, like that is going to protect me.

I catch her digging in her nose and then wiping her boogie on her skirt. She has the nerve to offer me some of her snacks before take-off. I want to vomit in my mouth. She is so bothersome. I know that she has no idea she is fucking with me. She is just trying to be nice, but she is irking me!

I start looking her up from head to toe. *Doesn't she have someone to help her get dressed?* She has on a denim knee length skirt with nude knee highs. She has on black flat walking shoes with white laces! The laces look brand new like she just bought them. This actually makes it worse.

Miss Jenny, who I learn is a retired school teacher, has on a red, white and blue button up plaid shirt. She also has on an old-looking linty brown cardigan sweater that has a couple of stains on it. Her hair is very white and must have an entire bottle of hair spray in it. All of her hair is sculpted into a dome on top of her head. It is very thin and I can see that she is balding in the crown area. This is probably why she has the cone-head hairdo.

She has on maroon colored drugstore reading glasses with some of the sticker still on the left side close to her ear. As I notice the sticker, I notice that she has some built up wax in her ear peeking out at me. I am so turned off by this overly-nice lady. Honestly, all she is doing is trying to be friendly. I am not having it though. She wants to know all of my business. I keep

giving her one-word answers, hoping that she'll catch the hint.

Either she doesn't catch it or doesn't care. She talks to me non-stop the entire flight.

Richard is asleep. So he has no idea what is going on. I keep looking at my watch dying to get off

of the plane. I pray that we don't taxi a long time once we finally land. When it looks like Miss

Jenny is getting sleepy and is about to doze off, the damn pilot, with his loud-ass mouth wakes

her up with his sales pitch for signing up for dividend miles credit card.

Now I'm pissed, but at least the flight is almost over. Miss Jenny is telling me about her

grandkids and how one of them is into drugs, but the other one is into real estate. She is

actually coming from her condo that her "good" son encouraged her to buy. She is going down

to Charlotte for the winter and will return to Massachusetts sometime after May. Her condo

will be vacant. Just then it occurred to me that God must have sat me on the plane next to this

woman to bless me and here I am damn near blocking my blessings.

Miss Jenny and I exchange numbers by the end of the flight. I make arrangements to

meet with her next week to discuss the terms of renting out her condo and she is going to give

me a damn good price. She says that I will be doing her a favor by renting it. She won't have to

worry about it throughout the next two seasons.

Richard sleeps the entire flight. I tell Miss Jenny all of my business about getting a job

and even tell her about the way Richard's family isn't too keen on welcoming me into the

family. Miss Jenny is a sweet lady after all. She may have some nasty habits, but her heart is huge. That nasty ass perfume doesn't smell as bad by the end of the flight. It almost smells like roses.

When Richard wakes up, I give him a dirty look. He knows I'm mad because he slept the entire flight. He knows I can't sleep on planes. He is supposed to keep me company. I told myself that I was going to read my new book by Vick Breedy on this flight. The woman that recommended it said that it is really juicy. That's just my type of book. The type of book that makes you hurry up and turn the motherfucking page! I guess I will read it on the flight back to Boston.

My plans were to tell Richard about my job and my upcoming move to Boston while we were on the plane. I guess it will have to wait until we get home tonight. I hope this goes well. I really don't want a long-distance relationship. I want him to move out to Boston with me. I'm not sure if he is into me enough to move. I mean he doesn't have to move right away. I will do the long distance thing for a little while, but that shit will get played and I will want someone that I can be with that I don't have to take a plane to get to.

Finally we get home. I want to talk to him and he all of a sudden has a funky attitude and doesn't want to talk. He asks if it can wait. I want to say "NO IT CAN'T WAIT" but I say ok and put it off until tomorrow. I've been putting it off for this long. What's one more day gonna hurt? The time just flew by. Everything happened so fast. One minute I am getting my GED and applying for jobs and the next minute I am in Boston interviewing for a job I had no intention of getting or taking. Now, here I am employed and moving to Boston with hopefully a nice condo off of Mass Ave for below market rent, thanks to Miss Jenny.

Miss Jenny emails me just like she said she would. She shows me the pictures of the condo. She says it is furnished and looks just like the picture. To my surprise, the pictures look good. The inside was very modern. Well, at least the pictures of the inside space were modern. Miss Jenny didn't seem like a neat freak. I'm sure that I will have to do a lot of cleaning and disinfecting once I get there.

I email Miss Jenny back and confirm things. In her email to me she tells me that we can meet next weekend and I can pick up the key, sign the lease and make my first payment to her. I'd been saving and was planning on giving her three month's rent; since she was giving me such a good rate. I am going to be paying Charlotte rent in a Boston condo. Unheard of! Thank you God! I am thinking about calling out of work or just quitting, but I need the extra cash and don't want to leave on bad terms. Lord knows that I really felt like just giving them the finger and bouncing.

Richard goes to bed and I feel like leaving. His attitude was funky before he went to bed and he doesn't want to talk about it. Once he goes to sleep, I decide to go home and spend the night with Gina. I've been going back and forth between my house and Richard's for a while now. Richard tried to make his apartment feel like home for me, but it never did. As shady as my own mother is, sharing a space with Gina feels more comfortable than with Richard.

When I get home it is close to midnight. Gina is up talking on the phone in the living room. I have an idea of who she is talking to because it is about work. She must be talking to Brenda from Wal-Mart. Brenda works the same shift as she does, but they work on alternating days most of the time. They like to get each other caught up with the gossip that is going on at

Wal-Mart. Gina just gives me a head nod when I walk through the door. She doesn't want to disrupt her conversation, I see.

I go straight into my room. I get my house coat and head to the bathroom to take a shower. Once I get into the shower, I start thinking about my day. Then I start thinking about my past week. Then I start thinking about what's to come. My life has changed so much in the last few months. I went from working at Wal-Mart with no high school diploma to having my GED, a condo and a job in Boston.

I get out of the shower and step into my Adidas flip flops. I wrap my white terry cloth robe around me and head into the living room. I notice that Gina is still on the phone. I interrupt her conversation and tell her that I will be moving out. She says ok and continues her conversation. She doesn't even ask where I will be going. I don't bother to tell her where I'm going either. I guess I'll send her a fucking post card. You'd think a mother would put up more of a fight when her only child leaves the home for good. Not Gina. The way that she acts one would think she is my foster mother instead of my biological mother.

Gina always seems a little detached from me. I always feel like a burden and an inconvenience to her. She isn't the type of mother to show affection. She doesn't give hugs or kisses. I can't say that I ever remember her hugging me. Gina has been distant towards me my entire life. I always try to please her, hoping to get praise, hoping to make her happy. The most that I get from her is "you aren't as dumb as I thought you were."

I leave the living room and head to my bedroom. When I get there, I look at myself in the mirror and smile. Life is changing for the better. I am not going to be like my mother. I'm

95

smart. I have a conscience and a good heart. I am responsible and I'm going to make something

out of my life. I will not be like Gina. Maybe, I am like my dad. I will never know. Gina told me

that he died. I wish I got a chance to meet him. Even if he is a woman-beating pimp like Gina

says.

Maybe that's why she always felt some kind of way about me. How could she love her

pimp's child? How could she give hugs and kisses to the offspring of the man that made her

suck other men's dick for chump change? How could she love the child of the man that beat her

when she wasn't bringing in enough money from turning tricks? I was a constant reminder of

the past that she was trying to forget. I never really thought about it on that level. I was just too

consumed with how horrible of a mother she s for not showing me love. I fall asleep with this

on my mind.

I can't move. My body feels weak and I have little energy as if I'm drugged. Then all of a

sudden, a child is leaning over me trying to suffocate me with my head wrap. He has brown skin

and straight dark brown hair. He is skinny. He looks like he is Middle Eastern. I can't escape him.

He's not strong enough to successfully suffocate me but he is determined to do it. My body is

slowly regaining strength, but I am still struggling. Under normal circumstances I could easily

get up and move this child off of me.

Something is wrong with me. Why am I in slow motion? He is determined to take my

breath away. Who is this child and why is he trying to kill me? How did he get into my room and

where the hell is Gina? I can feel my heart beating faster and faster. I am about to panic. I can't

yell or scream because my voice has decided to stop working. I feel defenseless. I'm going to die.

Just as I decide to just give up and let this child take my life away, I wake up. I'm sweating and I'm afraid. I remember the dream as if it wasn't a dream at all. Then I start praying. There must be some evil spirits running around in this house. Prayer is the only defense I know against evil spirits.

That dream was just as scary as the dreams I sometimes have where I wake up in my dream and I'm paralyzed. I can't move at all or talk. Those dreams really do a number on me. No matter how hard I fight, I can't win. It's only when I decide to stop fighting it that I wake up out of those dreams.

I'm definitely scaring myself more than I should. It's three a.m. I'm up thinking about a demon-child spirit running through the house. I'm scared to go back to sleep. It's like it was a horror movie. I wonder what this dream was about. I wonder what the kid represented. I wonder why he was trying to kill me. I turn on the TV and decide to watch HGTV. I won't be going back to sleep any time soon.

I guess I was able to go back to sleep because I wake up and feel like I need to do something. I feel like I am late for something. I know that I don't have any appointments coming up, but I feel like I've missed something. I just can't figure out what it is. I sit still for about two minutes to try to see if something that I am missing comes to mind. It doesn't. I decide that I am just tripping and get up to get dressed for the day. Today I will be telling Richard that I am moving to Boston. Let's see how this conversation goes.

My phone rings and it's Richard. He must have sensed me thinking about him. I ask him if he has some time today to meet so that we can talk. He says no. I'm caught off guard by this. I then ask him when he will have time to meet. He says that he doesn't know. I see his attitude that he had from last night hasn't gone anywhere.

Now, I'm starting to get an attitude. If he doesn't want to talk about it I'm not going to make him. He's a grown man. If he has a problem, he needs to open his mouth and express it. I guess we won't be talking about my move today. I ask why he called. He said that he was just checking on me because when he went to sleep I was right beside him. When he woke up, I wasn't.

I have no idea why he is acting funny all of a sudden. I'm not going to beat my brain and try to figure it out either. I'm trying to make moves. I got other stuff to deal with that requires my attention instead of dealing with his moody ass. I swear! Sometimes it's like I'm dealing with another bitch. Well, I don't' have time for any of that today.

Ava:

I'm at the gynecologist's office and she's doing a breast exam. I know that she feels something because the exam takes longer than it usually does. She tells me that she is going to refer me to an oncologist to get further examined. She said that she doesn't want to scare me, but she is all about being proactive.

She said that she knows that I'm going to be stressed until I find out what's going on with my body. So she had her office assistant set the appointment up with the oncologist for later today. All I had to do was show up. It was hard enough coming to this appointment. I worked up the nerve and now I have to have anxiety about seeing the oncologist. Everyone knows you see an oncologist when you have cancer. Why didn't she just come out and say that she thinks I have cancer? Let's just get this shit over with.

I still have a few hours to kill until my appointment. I decide to do some shopping. Shopping is a good distraction and it always makes me feel better. As I walk into Coach—still one of my favorite stores—my eyes are instantly drawn to a fuchsia-leather handbag. I pick it up without looking at the price tag. If I like it, I'm getting it regardless of the price. It couldn't be any more than five hundred dollars.

An hour later, I walk out of Coach with three handbags, a few belts and a scarf. Only one of the handbags was for me. The other two were for my daughter Karma. She will love them. One is chocolate brown and the other is burnt orange. I've been shopping at Coach since I was a young girl. If I was smarter back then I would have bought stock in it. Ok, I still have an hour to kill until my appointment.

A Bitter Beat Down

Eve:

Richard is tripping. I don't know what I did to this fool but he is acting like a bitch for real. If he doesn't stop acting like he got a pussy instead of a dick, I'm going to leave his ass here and get me a new man in Boston. I tried to meet him for lunch today and he said he was busy, I then asked when he would have some time and he said he didn't know.

I'm going to give him a few days to stop sulking and talk to me about whatever is bothering him. I hate it when folks got something going on with them and then they want you to work extra hard to get them to say what's bothering them. Just spit it out already! I'm that bitch that will just say "to hell with it" and let you work it out on your own. That is too much catering in my opinion. He should be catering to me when it comes to dealing with emotional shit, not the other way around.

I have the day off. I decide to do some shopping to prepare for my move to Boston. The weather is definitely different in Boston. So I actually need clothes for four seasons. I definitely need a heavy jacket or coat. Massachusetts gets snow!

After I find a nice Calvin Klein wool pea coat—which was very hard to find in Charlotte— I head to Forever 21. I see a couple of cute dresses that I want to try on. As I'm giving the clothes to the sales person to count, I hear someone talking shit behind me. I'd know that voice anywhere. I didn't even bother to turn around.

The fitting room attendant hands me back my clothes and I walk into the fitting room. Lynn's out there still talking shit loud enough for me and anyone in the fitting room to hear her. She's out there with her cousin, the one that I can't stand. I start talking to myself in an effort to calm myself down. I really want to go out there and whoop her ass again.

I can hear the fitting room attendant asking them to refrain from using that type of language in the store and threatened to call security. Lynn is definitely begging for me to beat her ass. She is talking all types of shit out there with her cousin. I continue to try on my clothes, but I am not in the shopping mood anymore.

I walk out of the fitting room and hand the attendant all of the clothes I brought in. I am not buying any of them. I was going to call Richard to tell him what just happened, but then I decide against it. I walk to the food court and grab a chicken Caesar salad wrap to take home. I walk through the door that opens to a corridor that leads to the exit. It's one of those side exits that mall employees use when they get off of work.

It's empty. I think to myself that someone could get raped in this long ass corridor. I'm halfway to the exit and I hear the door behind me open. I continue to walk towards the exit. Then I hear:

"What's up, Eve?"

I turn around to see if she is by herself or if her cousin is with her. As I expected, her cousin is there right by her side. So I respond to her by saying, "What's up, Bitch?" I drop my purse because I know it's about to be on. I know that her cousin isn't going to let the fight be fair. I don't have anything inside my purse to make this fight unfair either. The only thing that I

have that could possibly serve as a weapon is a pen. I don't have enough time to even consider

going inside of my purse.

She runs down the hall and tries to rush me. She didn't have to do that because I wasn't

going anywhere. I am ready to fight her again. To my surprise, it's only her. Her cousin is video-

taping us on her phone. I guess the fight was going to be fair after all.

Lynn is tall. So when I go to punch her, I punch her dead in her neck. She tries to knock

me down, but I don't fall easily. The punch to her throat stuns her. She puts her hand to her

neck as if she can't breathe. I take that opportunity to go in on her. I punch her in the eye. I

punch her in the gut and then I use a cardio kickboxing move and drop-kick her ass. She falls to

the ground and doesn't know what hit her. Now her cousin drops her phone and runs after me.

I don't have enough energy for another fight, but I say what the heck. Me and her

cousin go at it. She gets a few good hits in. I see she is trying punch me in my mouth. I guess she

wants me to have a missing tooth like her cousin. I am not going to let that happen. Shiiiiiit, I'm

too young to be wearing a bridge in my mouth. I turn my head every time she tried to hit me in

the mouth. She got me in my eye one good time. After that, I lost it.

I start punching her in the face repeatedly. I don't stop until she is bloody. I hear one of

the corridor doors open. Lynn's weak ass is still stunned on the ground. This couldn't have

lasted more than two minutes, but it felt like thirty minutes. I grab my purse and run out to my

car. I don't look back. I don't need any more court dates. I make sure that I grab Lynn's cousin's phone before I leave. I don't need any evidence that can lead me back in jail. I never want to go

back there. Believe that!

I look in the rear-view mirror and I can tell my eye is going to be fucked up. I bruise

pretty easily as it is. She could have just flicked me with her finger and I would have bruised.

Now imagine the damage that a good punch will do. I guess I am going to have to leave Wal-

Mart on bad terms. I am not going in tomorrow or any other day. It was definitely time for me

to get out of Charlotte. My court case for my first fight with Lynn is at the end of the week. I

wasn't going to go, but now I figure I better go so that I don't have anything hanging over me. I

need to make a clean break when I leave Charlotte.

I get off with a suspended sentence. If I fuck up again, I will have to do some time. I

think that was kind of harsh, but whatever. I don't plan on fighting her or anyone else any time

soon. I'm just trying to get out of Charlotte and start over. I met with Ms. Jenny this morning to

give her three month's rent up front and to get the keys to the condo. She decides to let me

lease it for a year. She said that she could stay with a relative when she came to Boston in May

next year.

I don't get a chance to meet up with Richard or talk to him this week. Enough is enough.

I'll be at his house tonight waiting on his ass to come home. He needs to stop acting like a bitch.

If he isn't feeling me anymore, I'm sure it has something to do with his family's influence. It is

obvious that they don't think I am good enough for him. Fuck them!

"What are you doing here?"

"Waiting on you, what do you think I'm doing here?"

"I already told you that I wasn't ready to talk, Eve."

"Well, when you gonna be ready, *Richard*?"

"Why are you in such a rush to talk to me? You going somewhere?"

Oh shit, he knows. "Why would you ask that?"

"Stop fucking playing games with me Eve. You and I both know you been keeping a secret."

Damn, how did he find out? "I don't have any secrets Richard." I was lying. I had plenty of secrets. I am not admitting to any of them until he comes out and says what he is referring to.

"I'm one second from calling you a lying bitch. You were going to leave and not say anything."

Ok, so he does know. I'm not sure how. The only two people that know are Gina and Ms. Jenny. I know that he hasn't talked to either of them. How did he find out before I got the chance to tell him?

"No! I've been trying to tell you! You've been dodging me since we got off of the plane." Then it dawned on me. The plane. He wasn't asleep while I was telling Ms. Jenny my business.

"Yeah, the plane, what an interesting trip back to Charlotte it was."

"Well, if you knew, you should have said something instead of faking like you were asleep."

"I've been thinking about this since we landed. You don't respect me enough to share significant events in your life with me. If you did, Ms. Jenny wouldn't have heard about it before me. I'm supposed to be your man. Instead you treated me like some random dude. What am I just a good fuck to you? I thought we had something deeper than that. Yo, I'm getting a headache just talking about this nonsense. "

"Richard, I'm sorry. I was trying to find the perfect time to tell you. Each time that I was going to tell you, something got in the way. I do respect you and I don't think of you as just a good fuck!"

"Yes, the hell you do, Eve!"

"No, the hell I don't. How are you going to tell me how I feel?"

"Well, it's clear you don't feel close enough to me to tell me about you moving to Boston!"

"First of all, lower your mother fucking voice."

"I ain't lowering shit!"

"We ain't having this conversation until you are able to talk to me with some respect."

"Respect? Bitch please! Respect went out the window when you told an old-smelly-white lady about your plans to move before you told your man!"

"Stop being so damn dramatic and stop playing games! If you heard what went down, why didn't you just call me on it instead of pouting like a biiiiiiiiiiiiiiiitch!"

"Oh, so I'm a bitch now? Ok, I will show you how bitches act. Get the fuck out of my place and kick bricks trick!"

That's exactly what I did. I left. I don't know that man. He is definitely tripping. Did he call me a trick? He had the nerve to get loud with me and shit. To think that I was hoping that he'd eventually move with me to Boston; that ain't happening. I realize that I let myself get talked down to and treated badly by his family for no reason.

I showed him no respect? I showed him enough respect not to go the fuck off on his mother when she was talking all that shit to me! He has a fucking nerve! Maybe it's better that things end this way. I will be starting a new life in Boston. He can keep his raggedy ass here in Charlotte. He can find a new "trick" to trip on. I'm not the one!

I head back home to Gina's. She's in the mirror putting on lipstick that is too dark for her complexion. She's listening to some old-school song by Mary J. Blige. I'm guessing she has a date because she has on a too-tight pink dress that shows every bump and varicose vein. She's trying to look young, but that dress just makes her look older. I'm not going to be the one to tell her.

When her date arrives at the door, instead of beeping from his car, I think to myself that at least he has some home training. Little did I know, he rang the doorbell because this fool took public transportation! I can't believe this shit. How you gonna pick up your date without a

car. He could have at least rented one or borrowed somebody else's. Soooo tacky!

Gina didn't seem to care. She asks him when the next bus to downtown is scheduled to

come. She doesn't want to miss it. He tells her that she has about ten minutes until the next

bus comes. She needs to hurry up. Not because her bus is coming, but because I'm in a foul

mood and her being in such a good one is fucking with me.

They leave and walk to the bus stop down the street hand and hand as happy as can be.

I go in my room and sulk for a little bit. I realize that not only am I losing Richard, I'm losing the

best dick I've ever had in my life. My expectations will be high for the next man. No doubt there

will be a next man. I hope he can handle his business as good as Richard. Every man will now be

compared to Richard. I know that's not fair, but once you've had good dick and I mean really

good dick, you never want the mediocre kind again.

I almost felt like crying, but I wasn't sure if I would be crying over Richard or his dick. I go

to the refrigerator and look for something to eat. I shut the door. I'm not going to get fat over a

man. Fuck that shit. He ain't worth all that! I walk out of the kitchen and head to my room. It's

dark. I turn on the light. It looks like someone was rummaging through all of my things.

That's exactly what happened. Gina was in here looking for an outfit. I have clothes all

over my bed and most of my drawers were open. This bitch was trying on all of my clothes for

her date with the bus-pass man. Now, I know where she got that dress. I didn't care though. It

wasn't mine. She took one of the dresses that I borrowed from Lynn and never gave back. . I

can't believe that we aren't friends anymore. I've lost my best friend and my man. There's no

107

reason to stick around. There's nothing for me in Charlotte. What's even more telling is that nobody even asks me what happened to my eye.

Ava:

Ok, so I got all types of tests run on me this week. Between the oncologist and my primary care physician, I feel like a guinea pig. I dodged a bullet with the oncologist. I don't have breast cancer. I have a cyst that they will remove next week. My PCP called me and said that my chest x-ray revealed that I have scoliosis. Some shit I wasn't even looking for. When I ask if there was anything that I can do about it, he said that it is just a slight curve and that I should make sure I stay active and exercise. That's easier said than done. My energy level has been at an all-time low.

All of my staff will be in the office tomorrow. They will be given their assignments during our first real staff meeting. Our meeting starts at eight a.m. I already know someone will show up late. I stressed the importance of being on time during their last interview. Let's see who paid attention.

I did some research on Eve. She has been living in Charlotte with some chick named Gina for her entire life. Gina claimed her as her own. Eve has no idea that Gina is not her real mother. She has no idea who her father is and that he is in Boston. I know that it was God's doing that she applied to my job listing. He's giving me a piece of Charlene back.

Eve is the first one to arrive at the office. She is there at seven thirty a.m. That's what I like, someone that is serious about their paper. Karma is here because she drove in with me. I instruct Karma to show Eve what cubicle she will be in and remind her that we have a staff meeting this morning. Karma says ok and brings Eve to her cube.

I plan on having Eve work on Lance's case with me. I will be handing out case assignments this morning. Each of them will start off with two cases. I will keep the caseload at two to make sure that they give the proper time and attention to each case. When they are able to handle more cases, I will assign more.

One by one, my staff start arriving. The last person arrives five minutes to eight. She was cutting it close. I bet she will be the one that has a time management problem. Karma does her job and shows them all to their cubicle. She's doing a good job. I won't accept anything less from her. She knows this.

We are all sitting in the staff office. The office is mediocre in size but the furnishings make up for it. The walls are pale gray with white bead boards on the bottom half of the walls. The ceilings are tray ceilings that are painted ivory.

All of the chairs are leather Coach boardroom chairs. The boardroom rectangular table is white and gray marble. I have a glamorous crystal chandelier that falls right into the center of the table. Placed in front of each employee is a Mac computer.

I take this opportunity to thank the staff for their interest and tell them that their interest is making it possible for me to fulfill the dream of owning my own private investigating agency. Then I get down to business. I explain the system that we will be using and instruct

them to become familiar with it. I tell them that the Macs are not to be used for personal

affairs. If it has nothing to do with Still Bitter Private Investigations, then they have no business

using it. They need to keep it in a safe place if they use it while at home. If it is in their car, it

needs to be in the trunk. They all nod in agreement.

Everyone gets their two assignments. They are instructed to take the entire workday

and study each case diligently. An hour before the end of the work day ends, we will regroup

and meet back in the conference room. Any questions that they have will need to be asked at

that time. Tomorrow they will be in the field investigating. I inform everyone that I will be

working with them on one of their two cases periodically. I thought that everyone would have a

problem with it, but to my surprise, they act relieved.

It's the end of the day. We've already had our meeting to go over any questions they

may have regarding their assignments. The first person that I will be working with on their case

is Eve. Once this case is resolved, I'd be working with Cocoa on her case. Cocoa is really a dude.

I think she thought that piece of information would be the reason why she didn't get hired.

Shit! That was the reason why I hired her. She will be my connect into that world. She will

definitely come in handy. I consider her my secret weapon.

Eve comes into my office before leaving for the day. She wants to know if she is

expected to come back into the office tomorrow to start on the case or somewhere else. I tell

her that I will meet her at her house. She looks at me funny and then quickly changes her facial

expression and agrees to have me over at eight a.m.

Eve:

Why this woman wants to come to my house is beyond me. I thought we'd meet at the office or in a public setting somewhere. She shocked the shit out of me when she said she'd be meeting me at my house. Good thing I got everything cleaned up and in order.

When I get home from work, I just want to relax. I did feel like soaking in the tub. I wasn't in the mood to be washing the tub out after I soaked in it. That may sound lazy, but I decided to just take a long hot shower.

The water is so hot that it stings, but at the same time it is soothing. I hope none of the steam finds its way under my shower cap. While I'm in the shower I start to think about things. I think about Richard. As mad as I am with him, I miss him. He was a constant in my life. Telling each other good morning and good night every single day was our ritual.

I have no one to call and say good morning to. Nobody is anticipating my goodnight call. All of a sudden, I feel sad. It's as if it is just now hitting me. It doesn't help that I'm all the way in Massachusetts. He couldn't come over to make me feel better even if he wanted to.

I start thinking about the strong physical connection that we have. As soon as his lips touch my lips, my body is ready to surrender. I get an involuntary chill as I think about some of the things he does to me in the bedroom, in the living room and in the dining room. I'm tempted to call him, but I won't. He's not thinking about me. If he was he would have called me by now. Why allow myself to want for someone that doesn't want me?

111

My attitude changes from yearning for him to being pissed off at him all over again. He didn't care for me as much as he said he did. If he did, he wouldn't have let me go so easily. I'm all the way up here in Massachusetts and I have no one. I have no one to go on dates with. He was my companion. If there was a function, he was the one that went with me. Special occasions were shared with him. He was the person that brightened my day and had me craving his company. Where the fuck is he!

This shit is really fucking with my ego and my heart. My heart hurts because I love someone that clearly doesn't love me. Love doesn't treat you like this. Love doesn't make you feel like this. I'm looking for that Corinthians-love next time around; that patient and kind love. My ego is bruised because I thought more of someone than they obviously thought of me. I really can't believe we aren't together anymore. I'm back to being single. It's time for me to stop thinking about Richard and move the fuck on. It's his loss.

I swear dudes must smell the scent of a broken heart and attack. I must have been hit on five times on my way to Dunkin Donuts. It was just a ten minute walk. I gave everyone the cold shoulder except for one guy. As I am crossing the street to go into Dunks, a rat was crossing with me; a rat not a mouse! I didn't see it until I went to step on the curb and it cut me off. I missed my step and fell trying to avoid this rat. I'm afraid of mice. So you know I was scared shitless when this dirty gray gangster rat cut me off.

As I am gathering my ass off of the ground, this good-looking dark-skinned man helps me. In Charlotte, folks are kind. I'd heard a lot about folks from Boston and kind was not the word that they were described as. Needless to say, I am shocked by his gesture. He asks me if am I ok and once I say yes, he goes on his way. I thought for sure that he was going to flirt with me.

I go inside embarrassed as hell because I know folks in there saw me fall. I order my hot cocoa and grabbed a corn muffin heated with butter. By the time that I get back to my place, I figure my cocoa will be just right and my corn muffin will be moist. As I am walking to my building's entrance, I am daydreaming about my food. By chance, I notice that same dude that helped me off of the ground walking into a business on the corner of my street.

Me and my nosey self walks past the business all extra slow to see what he is doing in there. To my surprise, he is working in there. It's a temp agency. I thought he was going in there to look for a job. I was pleasantly surprised to see that he was walking around like he owned the place. My bold behind decides to go into the temp agency and step to him. I think the fact that he didn't step to me earlier makes me want to see what he is about.

I walk inside and two chicks stare me up and down. I know I'm looking good, so there is absolutely nothing that they could even try to talk shit about. The two chicks that are grilling me are in there looking for a job. I decide to fuck with them. I walk right up to them and sit in between the both of them, while they are waiting to be called. There really isn't enough room, but I squeeze my behind right in between them anyway. I sit there like I have an appointment too. The one to my left is huffing and puffing like she has better things to do than to gain some employment. The one to my right is chomping and popping her gum like she has no home training. She's irritating the shit out of me. Just when I've had enough and was about to check this chicken head, she gets called for her interview. The low class hoe has the nerve to take the

STILL BITTER   Vick Breedy

gum she was chomping the hell out of out of her mouth and sticks it under the bench we were

sitting at. I mean for real, I thought only kids did that nasty shit.

Now I'm disgusted and ashamed to claim that she was one of my people. Had she been

of a different race, I wouldn't have felt so messed up about it. Chicks like her give chicks like me

a bad name. Now it's just me and the girl to my left. She's graduating from huffing and puffing

to complaining out loud like I'm going to join in the conversation.

We ain't girls. I don't know why she feels the need to look at me and say, "You feel me?"

Under normal circumstances I would have said "No Bitch. I don't feel you", but since I was in

here with an agenda, I just said "mmmmmm hmmm" and ignored her until she is finally called.

While I am sitting there ear hustling and watching folks like I am writing a book, he comes over

to me.

"The person ahead of you was our last appointment, is there something I can help you

with?"

"Actually, I wanted to know your name."

"My name is Neal."

"Aren't you going to ask me my name?"

"It's Eve."

"Ok, how the hell did you guess that?"

"You are still wearing a name tag from some type of networking event I presume."

"Oh!" I say and then peel off the sticky name tag with my name written with a green magic marker.

"So, again, is there something I can help you with?"

"No, I'm good. I've seen and heard enough. Thanks."

I leave him there standing dumfounded. Kinda like when he left me outside of Dunks, once I was off of the ground. I know where he works and now I know what time he goes for his last coffee break. This could be a nice distraction from the bullshit I'm dealing with. I plan on going to Dunks the same time tomorrow.

Ava:

Cynthia isn't doing any better. Craig is still on the hunt for the person who shot her. He has put all of his men on this and has called in a few favors. The person that did this wanted Craig to suffer. He's definitely suffering. The person that did this is going to suffer far more. Mark my words.

I pull up to Eve's place. There's no parking. I feel like crap. I've been having more days feeling bad than feeling good. Needless to say, I don't feel like hunting for a parking spot. I drive around the block four times until someone pulls out of their spot a few doors down from Eve's. Twenty cars go by before I can open my damn door to get out. I can't stand parking on busy-ass streets. Once I get out, I fold my side view mirror in so I don't have to bust somebody's ass for clipping it.

There's a homeless guy grilling me from across the street like he knows me. I want to say something so bad and believe me it wouldn't be something nice. I hold back because I remember that Law and Order episode where a homeless dude killed somebody and got off because he was mentally ill. I'm not trying to get killed today.

Somebody is walking out of Eve's building as I am walking in. I don't have to ring her buzzer because I am already in, but I do it out of courtesy anyway. She buzzes me in immediately without asking who it is. I am going to have to check her on that. She could be letting in a rapist for all she knows.

She must have heard my heels because she opens the door before I get a chance to knock. The place is nice. I'm not sure how she is swinging this but she must have gotten a hook up. I smile as I walk in and take a quick assessment. She's very clean and orderly. Everything had an assigned place. She takes pride in her possessions. You can tell a lot about a person when you observe how they keep their home. I won't eat food that someone has brought from their home, unless I've been to their home first and seen how they are living.

If they got cats running all around or dogs that they treat like family, I'm not eating from their house. No telling what the entitled dog or cat is doing while their owner isn't looking. If the person smokes, I'm not eating from their home. I don't know many smokers that wash their hands after every time they go smoke a cigarette. If their house isn't clean or they keep dirty dishes in their sink for too long, like overnight, I ain't eating food from their house. No telling what type of insects and rodents they got running around in their home. I'm not eating food

that their roaches got to sample first. Fuck that shit.

I tell her that she has a nice place. She tells me that the woman she is leasing it from

already had it furnished. She just rearranged the furniture and cleaned the place up. She leads

me into the open-concept kitchen. The kitchen is a soft yellow with white and pewter accents.

The counters are gray and white quartz. The cabinets are eggshell white with beautiful

hardware. The floors throughout the house were cherry wood. The entire house smelled like

apple pie and cinnamon due to the candles she had burning in each corner of the home.

I wait for Eve to sit down and she brings me a Dunkin Donuts covered coffee cup. It has

HC hand written on the side with black marker. This little bitch pays attention I see. Yesterday,

while I was at the office, I had hot chocolate from Dunks. She hands me a straw. She picked up

on that too. I don't want my teeth to become discolored. I only drink it with a straw. She is

getting all types of cool points.

She has her computer pulled up and she also has a note pad to take notes. I thank her

for the cocoa and we get down to business. I tell her what I need her to do this week and

instruct her to put her notes in every night because I will be keeping track of the activities that

she loads into our database. I tell her that no matter how unimportant the target's behavior

may seem, I wanted to know everything that she observed. I told her to report back to the

office on Thursday for our staff meeting.

Eve is very hospitable. She is kind. She is attentive. She has street smarts and I think she

will be one of my best workers. I left her home an hour later. I am not going far. Ironically,

Lance and his man live on the second floor of this building. I had to look at the address Eve gave me twice. I couldn't believe that Lance and Eve were living in the same building. She was shocked, too, when I gave her the target's address. I tell her to follow him to work and make sure that she follows him home from work. Lance told me what time his husband leaves home and gets off of work.

I am going over to Lance's this morning to bug his home. He doesn't know it. I know that he wouldn't have agreed to it, but if he wants to find out what's going on with his husband Javier, this is what I'm going to have to do. I knock on his door and Lance opens it. He is shocked to see me. I tell him that I was in the area. I just wanted to say "hi" before he went to work.

Lance is still training people, but now he has his own gym. He still looks magnificent. His body is perfect. He looks fifteen years younger than his actual age. I joke with him and tell him that he will be eighty years old looking like he's fifty if he keeps it up. I'm joking but there's some truth to it. As he's getting ready for work, he's walking from room to room talking to me in the process.

I manage to slip the bug in his husband's phone, on the house phone and I put one in Lance's cell too. I feel bad doing it, but it is necessary. I also manage to plant some surveillance devices in their home. I put one in the kitchen, living room, foyer and back door. I figured I didn't need to see what was going on in their bedroom or bathroom; although, the bathroom is where I caught my late ex-husband and his bitch. I will never forget that day. There's nothing like seeing another woman giving your man that killer head in the bathroom shower. They are dead and gone and I still get mad about that visual.

Karma:

My plan works like a charm. I maintain contact with him while my fake injury heals. I

have him anxious for our next date. Then I cancel on the day of. Believe me. I want to see him

real bad. These sex toys are getting played. I was ready for some real dick. I did my research

and his pockets are deep. His family has deep pockets. He was definitely getting this pussy. Ava

will be proud. After all she trained me for this.

Ray makes plans to take me away for the weekend. We are going to the Cape. His family

has a home located at Martha's Vineyard. I tell him that I'd love to go to the Vineyard for the

weekend with him. I then make myself unavailable until the weekend. I want him to not only

want me to come with him for the weekend, but I want him to hope that I am going to go with

him for the weekend. This is how I control this new relationship.

He calls. I don't send his call to voice mail. I let it ring and let it naturally go to voice mail.

I then listen to his voice mail and try to gage his emotions based off of his word choice. From

what I could gather, he sound like he really is looking forward to seeing me. That isn't enough.

He needed to sound confused and disappointed; confused by not hearing from me and

disappointed that he may not get a chance to spend the weekend with me. That's how I need

him to be.

I answer his call Thursday night. It's the night before we are supposed to leave. I explain

that I don't know his phone number by heart and that I dropped my phone causing it to fall into

the tub. It got ruined and I have nobody's number. I tell him that I am so glad that he called. I had no way of getting in touch with him because I lost all of the numbers in my phone. I tell him that I had to get a new phone.

By the end of our call, I have him right where I want him. I have one more tactic to use this weekend and then I will lay off the games for a while. If all goes according to plan, I won't need to play any games any time in the near future. Ray will be my man. He will be my first.

When I get out of work, Ray picks me up in his midnight-blue Mercedes SUV. I see Eva walking out just as Ray shuts the passenger side door. She is breaking her neck like she knows him or wants to know him. I can't tell. I will have to investigate that when I get back. That bitch can't know him. She just moved out here from Charlotte. Maybe she wants to know him. Shiiiiiiiiiit I don't blame her. She has good taste.

The weekend was great! I had such a good time. Ray is such a keeper. I needed him to feel like he was the lucky one. My last trick, no pun intended, is what sealed the deal.

I didn't know how freaky he was, so I had to feel him out. I couldn't just order him to eat it and start talking shit to him. I needed to learn him. So when he went to put on a movie, I excused myself to the bathroom.

When I came out, I'd let my hair down, took off everything except my red lace panties and black pointy high heels. I work out all of the time so I know my legs were looking right in my heels. I covered my breasts with my weave but my nipples were peeking through. I felt sexy and I know I looked sexy. I walked toward him but his back was to me. I asked him if he found what he was looking for. He answered me, but never turned around.

120

Since he was clueless, I figured I had to help him out. So I decided to use shock value. I casually told him that my pussy was wet and that did the trick. He turned around with the quickness. He saw that I was looking delicious. I know I shocked him with my nakedness. I knew I looked good. He just looked at me and didn't say anything. He walked over to me, kneeled down and ate me through my panties. That shit was good.

Then I went for the kill. I started talking real dirty to him and ordered him to put his dick in my pussy. His dick was hard like concrete and I was more than ready. When he put his dick inside of me I told him how good it felt. I told him how wet he was making me. He was getting more and more into it the more that I talked to him. I then straddled him. When he shut his eyes, I ordered him to open them and watch my titties bounce up and down. He liked that. I was riding him but he was giving it right back to me.

I saw his eyes glaze over a little bit. I knew he wanted to come. I knew he trying his best not to. So then I pulled out my last trick. We switched positions back to missionary. I needed him to feel like he was in control, but I really wanted to see how hooked I had him. I wanted to see his expression when I dropped the bomb on him. As he was pumping in and out of me, I lowered my voice and started telling him that my pussy was his. That made him get more excited.

I asked him how my pussy felt to his dick. He could hardly answer me. Then I asked him how it felt to have a pussy that ain't had no other dick but his? I didn't wait for him to answer. I started squeezing my walls tighter and tighter with each thrust. I then told him that I was about to come and his dick would be the first dick to ever feel me coming. That did it. He came before

I did. Knowing that no other dick has been inside of me did the trick. This man will love me

soon.

Ava will be so proud of me. She will approve of him. I know that she will want to hear

what went down play-by-play. Ray has deep pockets. He's a great business man. He's good in

bed and treats me right. Ava told me that I needed him to love me before I loved him. He needs

to love me more than I love him. That's the only way that I will be happy and keep the upper

hand.

Ben:

Jackie from Slade's needs some serious work on her head game. I am getting tired of

having to beat my shit after she sucks my dick to get myself to climax. Luckily, I met somebody

new that could give Ava a run for her money. The head is magnificent, but that's about it. I'm

not really attracted to this new one, but the oral skills make up for it. The swallowing makes up

for it too. This new one isn't someone that I'm going to flaunt around. A service is provided and

I show my gratitude by leaving a few C-notes and bounce. I make plans to get hit off again the

following week. I might as well schedule myself in through the rest of the year. It's that good!

I've been laying low, but some of my people have been telling me that Craig's been

asking around about me. This idiot could not have figured out that I had something to do with

it. He is either going on a hunch or his gut. He is one hundred percent right in trusting his gut,

STILL BITTER   Vick Breedy

but I'm not going to let on. Nobody but John and I know what really went down. John is on the

other side of the country out of Craig's reach. And I'm definitely not going to tell on myself. I

wonder how his bitch is holding up. I can't help but smile. I know this is driving that bitch-ass

motherfucker crazy.

When I get to the crib, I notice that I have a text message. When I open it, it's a picture

of my new jump off's lips slightly open as if they are ready to receive my dick. I think about the

head I just received by those soft lips and I get the urge to beat my shit. I grab the lotion and go

to work. My cum shows up within two minutes flat. I may see my new jump off sooner than I

planned.

I got things to do. I don't have time to take a shower. So I go to the bathroom sink and

wash my dick off real quick. I then head to the kitchen to grab myself a sandwich. I use the rest

of the lunch meat to make myself a ham, salami and cheese sandwich. I eat it on my way to the

bedroom. It takes all of four bites to finish the sandwich. I get what I need from the bedroom

and then leave the house.

Riding down Gallivan Boulevard, folks are driving like they have no motherfucking sense.

Dumb motherfuckers are driving like it's *not* raining outside. The roads are slippery. People are

driving above the speed limit when they should be doing the opposite. My phone indicates that

I have a voice message. I listen to the message and can't believe what I'm hearing! I get so mad

that I punch my driver's side window shattering it. Next time it will be someone's face and not

my window.

Eve:

Having the target live in the same building as me was ironic and convenient. My assignment was to follow this gay dude around to learn his routine. I was to do this every day. He takes the bus to work, so it is easy to ride the bus at the same time as him. I get off at the same stop as him. I know where he is going so I don't bother following him. I walk ahead of him. He wouldn't think that I was following him if I am ahead of him.

His building is a multi-company building. It is actually a mini-mall. He works inside of a tax preparation and accounting agency. I walk into his place of business and sign up to take classes to prepare other people's taxes. There are a few other people signing up. The classes start tomorrow. I will be here bright and early.

I decide to go back home, but not before I check out this boutique that is a couple of doors down from the tax prep agency. When I walk in, my nose is bombarded by the smell of cinnamon and chocolate. I don't know what type of candles they are using, but I definitely need some. The first thing that I ask the man at the counter is, "What is the name of the candle that you are burning and are you selling them?"

The man is dressed in a red and black plaid shirt that he had buttoned all the way to the top. He sure didn't leave much room for swallowing. On top of this plaid shirt, he has a yellow sweatshirt with a sketch of Rosa Parks on the front of it. The neck of the sweat shirt is cut as if

124

he did it to show off his plaid shirt. On his head he has a gray ribbed beanie. The gray of the hat matches his salt and pepper mustache and beard. When he comes from behind the counter to show me the candles that I am infatuated with, I notice he is wearing worn jeans and work boots. He is definitely a character.

The candle s called Cocoa Cinnamon Lust. He makes the candles! The label read Soul Vibe Candles. By the time I leave his store, I spend one hundred dollars. The boutique has everything that celebrates black people! There are candles, books, t-shirts, sweat shirts, paintings, incents, lotions, hair products, posters, figurines, flags, calendars, music, hats, gloves, bags and he even has bean-pies!

I end up buying a ton of candles. I buy the Rosa Parks sweatshirt he is wearing, but my sweatshirt is black. I buy a painting for my living room and some cocoa butter lotion. I really like this store. He is a nice guy. He didn't push any of his merchandise on me. He let me browse and ask questions while I browsed. He even gave me a little black history lesson while I was in there. I learned that he was a retired professor from one of the universities in the area. He told me his name but I forget it already. It didn't sound like a regular black last name. It's Van-der something. I'll ask him again when I come back.

I time it so that when I leave the store, I won't have to wait more than five minutes for the bus. As I'm standing at the bus stop, I notice my target walk right past me and go into the CVS pharmacy across the street. I decide to risk missing the bus and end up following him into the pharmacy. He grabs a copy of Ebony magazine and Positive Thought magazine. I am familiar with Ebony, but not as familiar with Positive Thought. I grabbed myself a copy of both to read

on my bus ride home.

The next aisle that he goes down is the cookie and chip aisle. He picks up a bag of sour

cream and onion chips. He then goes down an interesting aisle. I let him go to the register and I

slowly make my way to the check out. He buys chips, magazines, a lubricant and condoms. I

took a picture with my phone of his purchases. All that he was missing is some gum. His breath

was going to be kicking after he eats those sour cream and onion chips. I hope he has mints at

his desk.

He leaves and doesn't head back to the agency as I expected. Thank God I had a hunch

that this trip to the store was going to be worthwhile. The target went into the Marriott hotel

located a block away from CVS. I didn't go in. I didn't want him to catch on to me following him.

What I do is sit across the street on a bench as if I am waiting on the bus going in the opposite

direction. I read one of my magazines and patiently wait for him to come out.

This Positive Thought magazine is refreshing. It features entrepreneurs from the urban

community on the rise. I love it when those that deserve praise finally get recognized. There

aren't many magazines that celebrate the little guys making moves from the urban community.

This magazine is a resource for the person that wants to increase their hustle. Each person

featured tells their story about how they became successful. Each person's definition of success

varies too. It also talks about where they are going. This magazine is refreshing because it

captures entrepreneurs on their way up and not after they've already "made it."

I'm enjoying an article about Olde Soul Photography and I almost miss my target coming

out of the hotel. Just as I expected, he is out of there in less than an hour. I figured he was on

his lunch break and had to be back sooner than later. I do a quick inspection. His clothes look

neat. He didn't come out with anything extra that he didn't go in there with. What I did notice is

that he leaves without some of the things that he went in there with. All he had in his hand was

his magazine and his chips in his hand. The CVS bag, lubricant and condoms were nowhere in

sight. I take a picture of him leaving the hotel.

I sit at the bus stop and figure that I will see whoever he just had an encounter with

within five or ten minutes. He's gay, so I didn't have to pay attention to any of the women

exiting the building. I sat there for thirty minutes, only because I needed to wait on the next bus

going home. I took a picture of every dude, young, old, black, white, employee and guest. When

I get home, I'm going to look through my pictures examine the possible suspects. None of the

men that walked out were his husband Lance. I know what he looks like.

I'm home. I'm super excited about my candles. I can't wait to light them. I go into the

bathroom and light a Cocoa Cinnamon Lust candle. The aroma is intoxicating. The bathroom is

not that big so the scent is potent with the door closed. I turn the shower on and disrobe. My

plan is to take a nice long shower, put on my Jill Scott CD and de-stress. The hot steam mixed

with the scent of the candle coupled by Jill's voice did the job. I got out of the shower and felt

at peace.

I look at my naked body in the foggy mirror. My body is sexy. Even through the foggy

mirror, I look desirable. I think about Richard. He used to take showers with me. He'd lather me

127

up and massage my body parts in the shower. It would feel soooooo good. He'd have me weak.

I remember my knees actually buckling one time when he got on his knees and ate me while in

the shower. The water beating on my body with his lips and tongue exploring my pussy was the

most sensual experience that I've ever had. Damn I miss Richard.

I quickly try to shake that thought before I end up masturbating for an hour. I have work

to do. I need to find out who my target is fucking and not daydream about getting fucked by

Richard. I put on my terry cloth robe, my fluffy slippers and make some hot cocoa. I sit on the

couch and put my cocoa on the end table beside me. It's time to play detective. I narrow it

down to about three men. I then load my activities for the day into the job computer system. I

also upload the pictures that I took into the system. Ava wants to review everything daily.

Ben:

After I calm down a bit, I make a call to get my driver's side window repaired later on in

the day. I can't be riding around in a luxury vehicle with a broken window. I do have other cars

to drive, but I like to change my cars with my mood. So they all need to be available. The auto-

shop confirms that my car will be ready by this time tomorrow.

I make a phone call to John. That faggot-ass dude left me a message trying to get more

money out of me. He said that if he didn't get it, he had no problem going to the police and

turning himself in, but not before telling the police my involvement. He said that he spent all of the money that I'd given him and needs money to live day to day. He even had the nerve to say

that at least in jail, he doesn't have to worry about taking care of his basic needs. They did that.

I should have known this institutionalized motherfucker couldn't be trusted. I really ain't

worried about him turning himself into the police. They won't believe his ass anyway. What I

couldn't risk is Craig finding out about it. He has people in the police department working for

him. Even if they don't believe that I hired him to hurt Craig's bitch, word would get to Craig

that someone mentioned his bitch and he'll be investigating that shit like he is part of the CIA.

I send my jump off a text asking if tomorrow afternoon would be a good time to meet

up. Ten seconds later, I get a text confirming our date. My dick jumped just thinking about what

was gonna go down tomorrow afternoon. In the meantime, I make plans to send John some

money. I also make plans to kill that motherfucker. I just need to figure out how I am going to

do it.

Tomorrow couldn't get here fast enough. I meet my jump off at the hotel. I arrive first. I

decide to start masturbating just to get ready. We don't have much time because I got shit to

do and I need to take a car service to pick up my car at the shop.

My jump off knocks on the door. I was going to leave a key at the desk, but I didn't want

folks all in my business. I open the door naked with my dick in a salute. No words are

exchanged. My dick gets sucked while standing at the threshold. Anybody could have walked by

and saw us, but that made it that more exciting. I cum within two minutes and there's no proof

because it gets expertly swallowed.

My jump off then enters the room shuts the door and assumes the positon on the bed.

Face down and ass up. We handle our business. I definitely handled mine. I beat it up and

busted a nut. This sex is off the motherfucking chain. I never thought I'd meet someone that

could give Ava a run for her money, but my new jump off has Ava beat!

I arrange to have a car pick me up twenty minutes after my jump off leaves. I want to

have time to take a shower before continuing on with my day. Jackie calls me while I am leaving

the hotel. She wants to meet tonight. I decide that I've had enough for the night and tell her

that I will hook up with her tomorrow. She whines a little bit and then agrees to see me

tomorrow night. We are going to meet at Slade's on Tremont Street. I'm looking forward to the

meal more than I am looking forward to spending time with her. The mac n' cheese and fried

chicken is what will make my night.

John texts me and says that he got the money and he won't be bothering me again. That

dumb motherfucker has a habit. I'm sure he will be out of money again soon. The next time he

tries to pull this shit on me, I will have something for him. Next time the money will be

delivered with a poisonous snake in the bag to bite and kill his ass. He better stop testing me!

Karma:

"That's my dick!" That's what I scream to him while I'm riding Ray. He's loving it. He's in

love and I know it. I'm not in love, but I definitely enjoy his company. I could see myself loving him one day as long as he pays attention to my likes and dislikes, puts it down in the bedroom and is able to financially take care of me. Shit, if he does that, I will marry him.

Now that I've gotten a taste of dick, all pun intended, I was curious about new dick. Ray was good. He knows how to please me, but I want to try out different types of dick. I want white dick, Hispanic dick, Indian dick, Caribbean dick and maybe even some Asian dick. I'm not looking for a relationship. I'm in a relationship with Ray. I just want different dick.

I decide that I am going to sample as much dick as I want until I am no longer curious; until my appetite is satisfied. Of course, I can't tell Ray this. Plus, I don't want to lose him. He is definitely a good catch; marriage material. Right now I'm not looking to be a loyal wife. I want to be the freak that runs deep in my bloodline. My mom is a freak. Her mom is a freak and I'm sure my great grandmother was a freak too.

There's no way that my mom couldn't be a freak when she was giving me porn to watch and vibrators to use as a teenager. I mean who does that? She was creating a monster and she succeeded. Once I got some real-life dick, something inside of me went off and made me want sex all of the time. I want sex not just every day, but multiple times throughout the day.

I know that I wore Ray out during that weekend he took me to the Cape. I made him fuck me so many times that I think I might have scared him a little bit because he asked me if I had enough. When I said no, he thought that I was joking. When I didn't crack a smile, he gave me a concerned look. It's obvious that I want it waaaaaaaay more than he does. I don't want to scare him off or wear him out. So, let the hunt begin.

Getting dick is easy. When you look as good as I do, you have men begging to get a taste

of you. I want a taste of them too. That's exactly what I do. I taste and sample a different guy

every day of the week for two weeks. At the end of two weeks, I determine who I am going to

keep in my rotation to hit me off when Ray isn't.

The first guy that I did it with, other than Ray, is Hispanic. I felt a little guilty for cheating

on Ray so early in the relationship. I also figure that since we just started dating, he couldn't

expect us to be acting like we are married. My Latino lover knew how to tickle my bud just

right. It usually takes a little while for me to be satisfied when I'm getting head. This man has

me wanting to fuck after the first fifteen seconds. He is on my rotation list. He said he was my

Latin Lover, but I refer to him as my Latino Licker.

I figured three guys were enough. They were all a different flavor. The other man that I

have in rotation is a light-skin black dude. I'm not sure what he is. His name is what threw me

off. His first name and his last name are two first names. I don't think that he is plain black. He

might be Haitian or West Indian. I don't know and I don't ask. The only thing I want from him is

the dick. He earns his spot on the rotation list with his word game. This man knew all the right

things to say and could talk me right out of my panties. I think he said he was an author. We did

a lot a talking, but it was to make sure that upstairs is just as stimulated as downstairs. I call him

my Lip Service.

The last man on my rotation list is younger than the other two. He is Moroccan.

Technically he is black because he is from Africa, but he doesn't look black. He looks like Bin

Laden's crew. He's my age. He is finishing his freshman year in college. He is a star athlete for a

Division One college. I think he said that he goes to UMass Amherst. He's the starting point guard or something. He is fun to be around and he does whatever I demand in the bedroom. I like how he makes sure my needs got met and lets me boss his ass around while we were fucking. I call him my School Boy. He is someone that I can mold.

That is it. I keep three out of the fourteen. Don't get me wrong, Ray knew how to hold it down in the bedroom, but I want sex way more often than he does. He isn't always available when I need to be dicked down. And that's where my three sidekicks come into play. It is easy to go out with them unnoticed by Ray because he is always at one of his gyms. He is serious about his money and I love that about him.

I'm back at the office and Eve comes and sits down at my desk. I'm wondering what the hell she wants. We aren't friends like that for her to ask me about my weekend. So I am trying to figure out what this chick is up to.

"Karma, I noticed you had someone pick you up from work the first week that we all started working here."

"And?" I say to her with a hint of an attitude.

"And I wanted to know how you know that dude."

"Wow! You are moving pretty quickly. You know dudes from Boston already. Didn't you just move down here from Charlotte? How could you possibly know Ray?"

"So it was Ray?"

133

"Yah, his name is Ray. How could you possibly know him?" Now I'm getting heated.

"I don't exactly know him. I know his brother Richard."

"Now this I gotta hear!"

She goes on to tell me the story of how she dated his brother Richard. I believe her

because Ray told me that his brother lives in Charlotte. All I can say is small world. She tells me

a little bit, but I know that she is holding some stuff back. I don't blame her though. We aren't

exactly friends. It's kind of weird that we are both dating brothers. Well, let me rephrase that. I

am dating the brother of someone that she dated in the past. Ray told me that his brother was

dating his cousin's best friend and that she moved down to North Carolina to be with him. I

don't know if Eve knows this, but I decide to keep that bit of information to myself.

Eve:

As soon as I get to work, I sit down at Karma's desk. I know that was Ray she was with. I

want to know how she knows him. She wasn't at the family reunion. If she is dating him, it has

to be a new relationship. I know that she's going to be side-eyeing me as soon as I start to ask

her questions.

Come to find out, she's just as nosey as me. She won't give up too much info. I can tell

that she is keeping some shit to herself. I don't blame her because I do the same thing. It is definitely ironic that she is dating my man's brother. Correction, she is dating my ex-man's

brother.

Thank God for distractions. Lord knows that I'd be thinking about Richard every free

second of the day if I wasn't working and if I didn't have someone to go out on dates with.

Neal asks me out on a date when I bump into him again at Dunks. Of course, I accept.

Nobody else worthy was barking up my tree. I need to get Richard out of my system anyway.

Neal will definitely help me do that. I need some new dick in my life. Richard was good. I take

that back. Richard was great, but Neal might be better than great. I can't wait to find out.

I haven't had many jobs, but this job has been the best job of my life. I have a lot of

unsupervised time and as long as I get my assignments done, the boss doesn't bother me. Some

of these chicks don't know how to manage their time. I haven't really made any friends since I

have been working here. They keep to themselves and so do I. The only two people that I talk

to are the boss, Ava, and Karma. Karma just tolerates me. I know she hasn't been feeling me

since I purposely spilled her water. She'll get over it.

I'm meeting Neal at The Cheesecake Factory. I'm meeting him because I don't know him

well enough to get into his car. He's fine, but not so fine that I become stupid. The few

conversations that we have had on the phone have been ok. I hope they are better in person.

You really don't need a car living in Boston. You can take the orange line, red line, blue

line, green line or purple line wherever you need to go. I asked Karma for directions. She told

me to take the green line to the Lechmere stop and walk a few blocks to The Cheesecake

Factory located in the Cambridge Side Galleria Mall.

If she had have asked me, I would have asked her why she wanted to know. I guess she's

not as nosey as I am or she just didn't care. She gave me the information that I needed and

went on with her day. I still don't trust her, so I called the Cheesecake Factory and asked if

Lechmere was the stop that I should get off at. Karma might have thought she was cute and

given me the wrong directions. The hostess that answers the phone confirms that I have the

right stop.

As I'm getting ready to get dressed, I hear my stomach growl. I'm starving. I tell myself

to wait, because I'm going out in an hour to eat with Neal. I can't take it though. I have to get

something to eat. There are no frozen dinners in my freezer. They all got eaten throughout the

work week. There is cereal. I scarf down two bowls of Fruit Loops and instantly regret it. My

stomach goes from growling to crying. Milk and I have issues. I am definitely going to be

secretly pooting during this date.

I'm a little early. I scan the place to see if he happens to be here early too. To my

surprise, he's here. He stands up from where he's seated to make sure that I see him. We make

eye contact before he stands up. There is really no reason for him to stand, but whatever. I walk

over to him and I size him up. I only see him in his work clothes. I wondered how he dressed

casually.

He's wearing straight leg jeans that have a light-blue finish to them. On his feet he has

dark-brown Polo boots with a rubber sole. His V-neck Polo sweater is khaki-colored with a baby

blue Polo symbol that is fitting him just right. I'm able to see more of his physique. I can't see his belt, but it better not be black. He will lose so many cool points if he has on a black belt with brown boots.

Once I get within arm's length of him, he hugs me. I wasn't expecting a hug. He smells really good and the hug felt better than I would have anticipated. The hug felt so good I didn't want him to let go. That has to be a side effect from not having any companionship since Richard. If a hug made me feel that good, there's no telling what the dick could do for me. Here I go, already thinking about the dick and haven't even completed our first date.

"You are beautiful, Eve."

"Thank you. That comment caught me off guard."

"Really, why?"

"I mean, I'm really not dressed up or anything. Beautiful might be a stretch."

"Eve, your beauty is deeper than your attire."

"Well, again, thank you, Neal. Have you thought about what you want to eat?"

After I asked him about what he wants to eat, he notices that the conversation is making me feel a little awkward. That doesn't stop him from just looking at me and not answering my question, which created an awkward silence. If anything, Neal is interesting or maybe he's weird. I'm not sure yet. I *am* sure that I will know soon enough.

This man is a talker. He talks non-stop the entire time we are at The Cheesecake Factory. The only time he doesn't talk is when he is eating or drinking. He did warn me that he was a talker beforehand. I just thought that he was playing. The only good thing about it is that

everything he says is either interesting or entertaining. When he realizes that he left very little

room for me to add my two cents, he tells me that he promises he'll let me talk on our next

date.

He assumes he is getting a next date. I never told him that he and I would be going on

another date. How does he know that I like this one enough to go on a second? I would

appreciate being asked out on another date rather than being told that he was getting another

date. I was going to leave it alone, but I couldn't.

"Who told you that we were having another date?"

"Your body language told me."

"What the fuck is that supposed to mean?"

"Fuck, huh?"

"Ok, I am totally lost. I asked you what that's supposed to mean and you say "Fuck, huh?

What is up with you? I don't get it or you?"

"I said "Fuck, huh?" because I thought that it was interesting that you chose that word.

You could have used hell or even heck, but you chose fuck. We weren't in a heated discussion.

Your word choice confirmed what I already knew."

"Please stop talking in riddles and answer the damn question."

"I knew that I was getting a second date when I told you the story about my boy that's in an open relationship."

"How could you possibly have determined that you were getting a second date? I'm still lost."

"When I started explaining to you how an open relationship works for him and wouldn't work for me, your facial expression changed. It softened. You thought I was going to come to you with that bullshit. You were expecting me to say some shit like "man wasn't created to be monogamous." When I started telling you how I felt about making love and how I would take pride in intimately pleasing my one woman, you shifted in your seat. Even the way that you looked at me changed."

"I think you are reading too deeply into my body language."

"Don't be ashamed. I know that you shifted because I made that bud throb. If it wasn't our first date, I'd take care of that for you. I don't want you to be mad at yourself for giving it up on the first date. So I will wait for the next date. Maybe on that date, you'll let me feel how wet I make you. You want me to feel it. You just got too much pride to tell me. That's ok, though. I want to feel it and I will soon enough."

This idiot has lost his mind. He has a lot of nerve even speaking to me like that. He saw me shift. So the fuck what! A bitch can't shift in her seat without someone thinking that they are making her wet. This motherfucker is arrogant. The messed up part about it was that I enjoyed it. I like the shit he was talking and secretly hope he talks shit under the sheets. If he pays that much attention to my body language, I know he will pay attention in the bedroom. He

is right. My panties are soaked. Had he made a move he could have gotten it. I don't give a fuck

about it being the first night. He clearly doesn't know who he is dealing with. And yes he will

find out just how wet I can get when I sit on his chatterbox next time I see him.

Karma's Addiction

Karma:

I can't wait to be finished with work today. I've been talking to Lip Service in between

calls all day. He damn near had me wanting to masturbate at my desk! I originally agree to let

him pick me up after work so that we can get something to eat and then go back to his place.

Ten minutes before it was time to leave, I get a call from School Boy. I agree to meet him at his

dorm while his roommates are gone. That means that I have to skip dinner and get straight to

business with Lip Service.

By the time Lip Service and I are done, I have about thirty minutes to spare. I'm in my

car contemplating if I really have enough time to get home, shower and make it to the dorm. I

decide to skip the shower and head right to the dorm. I should have taken a shower before I

left, but it is too late now. As I'm driving to School Boy's dorm, Ray calls.

140

I'm silently praying that he hasn't made any plans for us tonight. He told me that he'd

be working late. I figured I'd take that opportunity to play. Now, he's on the phone telling me

that he'd be done sooner than expected and wants to have a late dinner with me. He tells me

where we'll be dining and I tell him that I will meet him there instead of him picking me up.

Thank God that my outfit for work was appropriate to go out dining. All I need to do was

remove the jacket.

I get to School Boy's dorm and I notice he did as he was told. I called him after I hung up

with Ray and ordered him to have the shower going and his dick hard by the time I got there.

He opened the door and all I could see was his beautiful Moroccan dick. I was so turned on by it

that I almost said to hell with the shower, but that would be nasty on my end. To go from one

dick to another without washing the juices off of me would be foul.

I get into the shower and clean off what Lip Service left behind. As I'm rubbing the soap

over my body for the second cleaning, I start thinking about all of the things I just did with Lip

Service and I feel myself getting hot all over again. I yell to school boy to come into the

bathroom. He does as he's told. I then open the shower door so that he can see my naked-

sudsy body. He thinks I'm going to tell him to come into the shower. I can tell because he's

taking off his watch. I stop him.

I really just want to fuck with him. I am going to give him a show in the shower, but not

let him touch me. At the same time, I want him to give me a show and stroke his dick until he

climaxes. He's young, so, I am not worried about him not being ready to go another round after

I get out of the shower. As I watch him, I rub my breasts slowly. The water was hitting my back as I was putting soap on the front of my torso. That water beating on my back combined with the way the suds were dripping down the front of my body felt good. What makes it even better is watching School Boy get turned on. I start fucking with him and tell him that he is taking too long to climax. I order him to beat his dick faster. I tell him that if he doesn't come right this minute, he isn't getting any of my good pussy. Then I slide my finger inside of myself. As soon as I withdraw my finger, I lick it. As soon as he sees that, he ejaculates all over the floor and the shower door.

By this time the water is losing its heat, I knew that the temperature wouldn't matter once I had School Boy in here with me. I let him clean himself off in the sink while I washed the suds off of me. I then tell him to get in the shower with me and beat it up from the back. I get turned off for a second when he enters the shower without a condom. What the hell is he thinking? I am not trying to die for the dick. I order him to get out and get a condom. He reluctantly gets out of the shower and gets one.

I am on a tight schedule. I have to meet Ray for dinner soon. I have a lot of things that I want to do with School Boy outside of the shower, but we are going to have to save that until next time. Ray already left me a message stating that he was in route.

I definitely welcome dinner. I am starving and have worked up an appetite. When dinner is over and we finally make it home, I get ready for round three. Ray should be thankful that I had my fix earlier or else he'd have to do me all night. He's usually done after two rounds back to back.

I'm back at work and I'm tired as hell. I didn't get home until two in the morning. I didn't actually fall asleep until three. Now I'm back at my desk struggling. Eve walks in all chipper and shit. She greets me with a hot cocoa from Dunks and bought donuts for the office. I'm wondering why she's so happy.

"What's up with you? Why are you so happy this morning?"

"I met a guy."

"Oh, is this the person you were going to meet at The Cheesecake Factory?"

"Sure is. We had phone sex all night and I can't wait to see him again tonight."

"I really didn't need all of that information. You could have just left it at you had a good time."

"Listen, I don't have any friends here. The best friend I had back at home slept with my ex-boyfriend. Then she and her cousin tried to jump me. My mother hasn't even checked in on me since I've been here. With all of that being said, I'm sorry. I don't have anyone to tell good news or bad news to. You and your mom are the only ones that speak to me. Since your mom is my boss, I figure it won't be a good idea to share my after-hour activities with her. So, you are the lucky winner."

After about five seconds of awkward silence, "Well, lucky me!" I say with a chuckle that follows.

Our relationship changed from that point on. Eve is warming up to me and I am definitely warming up to the idea of gaining a new friend. My mom encourage me to have a lot of friends, but it just didn't work out that way for me. Girls don't like me. I had a group of female friends all the way through middle school. Then one summer me having a group of friends turned into me having no friends. That memory is so vivid in my mind. I had just completed eighth grade and was having a sleep over with five girls from my school. Four of the girls that were invited I'd been friends with since elementary school. The fifth girl was a cousin of one of the girls. She was staying with her for the summer. So it was kind of a package-deal invite.

We all had a good time. The night was coming to an end and we had just finished playing Truth or Dare. My mom was gone all day. I figured she may stay out all night. I preferred that because every now and again she would say something that embarrassed the hell out of me when I had company. Unfortunately, she didn't stay out all night.

She came into my bedroom while we were all up talking about going to high school next year and the boys that would be there. She caught the tail end of the conversation and decided to chime in.

"All those boys at school are gonna want from you is pussy. It's ok to let them eat it, but don't give them any. Have your fun. You can let them finger you, but don't let them go any farther than letting them lick the kitten. Save it. Believe me, the boys in high school will not be the men you marry."

Then she exited without saying goodbye; the same way that she entered the room without saying hi. It was as if she was on stage, then dropped the microphone and left. As one could imagine, all mouths were left hanging open. She'd said some embarrassing things before around company, but she never really took it that far. She usually saved those conversations for me. She didn't look like she had too much to drink. I think she just didn't give a fuck.

All summer, I got the cold shoulder from the group. Nobody was available to hang out. Nobody called me to see what I was doing. It was as if I was in friend exile. I was bored the entire summer, but it gave me a chance to get to know myself. It gave me a chance to define myself. It gave me a chance to get comfortable with being alone.

I later learned that my friend's cousin ran her big mouth to her aunt. I couldn't believe that she told my friend's mom what my mom said to us. The rumor was that my mother was teaching me to be a prostitute. My mom allegedly encouraged them to be prostitutes too. The word spread and nobody female wanted to be my friend. I got a lot of attention from the boys my freshman year. They all thought that I was going to let them hit it. It only made sense, since I was the high school prostitute.

I'm so glad to be out of high school. I put off going to college for a year and decided to just work for my mother. I needed a break. Not so much a break from the educational piece, but the social piece is what I needed a break from. So here I am, working for my mom and I'm on my way to making my first female friend since middle school.

145

Eve:

Seriously! I can't believe this bullshit. My period is not supposed to come until Tuesday.

Today is Saturday and that sneaky bitch showed up. She is such a hater. Mother Nature knew

that I was supposed to get some today. She's the biggest cock blocker!

DAAAAAAAAAAAAAAAAAAMN! I was dreaming about the dick. Now I gotta wait a week for it.

I was talking all types of shit too. He knew he was getting some next time we saw each

other. I don't even know if I want to waste my time seeing him. All I'm gonna wanna do is have

sex. Since that ain't happening, we may as well wait to see each other. I'm going to text him to

let him know that unexpectedly and prematurely my biological shut down has begun. That's

what I get for being too excited to act like a hoe. I was thirsty for the dick. He knew it. I knew it.

Surprisingly, he still wants to hang out. I really don't feel like it. I tell him maybe another

time. He acts like his feelings are hurt. He starts guilt-tripping me. He is trying to make it seem

like I am just using him for one thing. He told me that I was just like a dude. I had to laugh at

that one. I decided to let him come over and chill for a bit. We could order in because I no

longer felt like going out. It was as if all the symptoms of my cycle hit me at once. He better

hope he doesn't get cussed out. My tolerance is low during this time.

Oh my God! I had such a good time. I almost forgot that I was on my period. Neal is so

much fun. We played board games, ate junk food and watched the DVD series of the old-school

TV show Good Times. His favorite on the show is Michael. Mine is Willona. He said it figures

that my favorite would be her. I never asked what he meant by that because I already knew.

We make plans to meet next weekend for dinner and dick. I tell him we can skip the movie.

Last week sure flew by. I don't need to go into the office today. I can work from home. I

gathered some good information. I am going to have an answer to who Lance's husband is

creeping with soon. Shit. I already knew he is guilty. I just need to pinpoint who he is getting it

in with. I narrow it down to two men. One of the men he meets with every week is gay. The

other one isn't, but he sees him just as often. I know something shady is up with them. I just

don't know what.

Poor Lance, his husband is such a dog. I thought homosexual men would be a little

better than heterosexual men. Nope! Gay men act like whores just like heterosexual men. Men

cheat on men. Men cheat on women. They are some unsatisfying pieces of shit. I think about

my ex-boyfriend Vince. He wasn't shit then and he ain't shit now. I thought I did a good job

satisfying him. He proved me wrong. Then he took it to an asshole level and dealt with my ex-

best friend Lynn. Where's the loyalty?

I make a mental note to make sure I follow up on a hunch. I'm trying to connect the dots

between a man named Ben Ford and Lance's husband. Later on tonight, I will go into

distraught-girlfriend detective mode. I laugh to myself. There are definitely different levels to

this investigative shit. I am going to go the extra mile with this case. I found out that one of the

men that Lance's husband sees weekly is Ben. I'll see Ben tonight at Slade's.

I took it upon myself to follow Ben for two weeks. I devote all of my time to this. I stopped following Lance's husband and figured I'd connect the dots by following Ben. I am still not sure what the connection between the two are, but I'll find out tonight.

Although, my hair is already dyed blonde, I put on my white-girl blonde, long, straight wig. Pink is the color for the evening. I put on my leave-no-room-to-the-imagination pink and white polka dot skin-tight mini dress. I put on my silver strappy high heels and assess myself in the mirror. I look like a straight hoe. My make-up hasn't even been applied yet. I doubt that it would have made a difference.

It's getting late. For the last two weeks, Ben shows up at Slade's around eleven thirty p.m. and leaves before one in the morning. It's midnight. I put my Barbie-doll pink lipstick on and put some heavy eyeliner above my fake eyelashes. That's it. I'm done. I inspect myself one last time. Ben seems to like his women to look slutty. Tonight I'll be exactly what he likes.

The guard at the entrance to Slade's opens the door for me. He's all grins when he sees me. I pay him no mind. It's Calloway's night and they are charging ten dollars at the door. I reach into my silver clutch Steve Madden bag and hand the person collecting admission my money. I head to the bar and a Dominican bartender asks if I'd like a menu. I am hungry as hell. Tonight, I am on a mission. There will be no eating. I order a shot of tequila. I know what Patron does to me. I limit myself to one shot.

When I arrive, I make sure that I sashay myself over to the bar slow enough for everyone to get a good look. Even some of the bitches were looking. I made eye contact with my target. As expected, he smiled. Although, my back was to him, I could feel his gaze

148

undressing me as I make my way to the bar. I gulp down my shot and plan on paying the bill

and making my move on Ben.

I don't have to. My tequila is paid for by the gentleman sitting three tables away. This

will be easier than I thought. Ben paid for my drink. I turn around to look in his direction. He is

already on his way over to me. I break my rule and let him buy me another Patron. My second

round isn't a shot. I can feel that second drink creep up on me ten minutes into my

conversation with Ben

Ben is a good-looking man. He is older, but still good looking. He and I start chatting it

up. I should have listened to myself and stopped at the first shot of tequila. He is spitting

bullshit at me. He is trying to get into my panties. If I didn't have a greater purpose for engaging

with him, I may have let him.

Shit. Things keep getting in the way of Neal and I hooking up. We were supposed to

hook up last week. He had to cancel. Then we rescheduled and I had to cancel on him. I am

definitely in need for some sexual attention. I just might let Ben hit it. I can't say that I've ever

done it with an older guy. This can be my little mixing-business-with-pleasure secret. I'll get the

info that I need and get some dick in the process.

Ben takes me to the same hotel that he meets up with Lance's husband. He gets us a

room and I give myself permission to be a whore for the night. I didn't suck his dick. I wasn't

going to go that far so soon, but I let him kiss and lick my cat. I will say that it was the BEST I've

ever had. This man knew how to eat some coochie.

149

Right before we are about to fuck, we get a knock at the door. I'm pissed because the person banging on the door is claiming to be room service, but the knock seems too urgent to be room service. My instincts tell me that it's probably another bitch at the door. Ben yells through door. He tells them that he didn't order any room service.

I can see the bulge in his pants trying to escape captivity. I thought that his zipper was gonna split. That's how intense his erection appeared to be. Like I said, I went with my instincts. I tell him to see what they want, so that they will go away. In the meantime, I'm pulling my dress back down from being hiked up to my waist. I didn't bother getting undressed. After all, he has only eaten me. When I stand up, I am fully dressed. I have no panties to collect because I didn't wear any. All that I need to do was grab my silver clutch.

If something is about to go down, I need to be ready to bounce. I am not gonna be caught up leaving shit behind or trying to gather my shit while the bitch on the other side of that door goes off on me and/or him. When he opens the door, I hear a surprising conversation. I no longer need to do any more investigating. That knock at the door is a blessing in disguise

"What the fuck!"

"Oh, you surprised to see me baby?" a male voice says sarcastically.

"Get the fuck outta here. You don't want to do this!"

"No, I'm not going anywhere!" a male voice screams in a high pitched tone.

"Keep your fucking voice down."

"I want to see what young tramp with a tight ass hole you got in here!"

I hear a loud sound. It was as if someone punched a wall. I walk into the living room portion of the suite. I see a man knocked out cold. Ben looks at me as I'm walking out of the bedroom. He says nothing. Neither do I. I step over the man that solved the riddle. I walk over Lance's husband. His eye is going to be fucked up. I wonder how he's going to explain that shit to Lance. I'm so glad that I didn't fuck Ben. He likes boys. I would have never guessed that one. Case concluded; Lance's husband is cheating on him with Ben Ford. Thank God, I didn't give Ben my number. Thank God I only let him eat it!

I don't know if I will ever find a man that I will truly trust. I wonder if I will find a man that won't let me down. I wonder if I will find a man that will love me the way that I need to be loved. I wonder how long my silly ass will be wondering. Let me not get sidetracked. I had the info that I needed. I need to let Ava know. I'll add my notes into the company's system when I get home. Then I'll call Neal to see what he's up to.

Ben:

What a fucking night! Shit was going good. I had some young bitch in my hotel suite. I was about to tear that pussy up. Then shit started getting messy. My jump off shows up and flips out like the bitch that he is. I don't know what the girl in my bedroom heard, but after I knocked his ass out, she left. She looked at me like I wasn't shit.

151

That's the first and last time some shit like that will happen. I knew that my jump off

was catching feelings, but I told him that there was no room for a dude in my life. All he can do

for me is suck my dick and shut up about it. Since he showed his ass tonight, I am gonna tell him

to beat it. That's exactly what I do.

When he regains consciousness, he tries apologizing. He want to make it up to me. He

offers to suck my dick. I let him, but he didn't know this will be the last time he gets to slobber

on my shit. I am disappointed that I missed out on getting some young pussy. In my head, I was

thinking of the lyrics from that old song by Plies *"Fuck that pussy. Give me that throat!"* I am not

going to cum in his mouth tonight though. Tonight he deserves to be punished.

I slip on a condom and I wear his ass out. Literally. He is screaming just like a bitch. That

shit is turning me on. I know that I am hurting him, but knowing that, turned me on more. Once

I am done, I wash my dick off in the sink with some warm water and hotel soap. He is smiling

like things are good between us. I walk over to him and start choking him. I do this before I

even button my pants. I tell him that if he ever steps to me again or even acts like he knows me,

I'll kill him. Then I release his neck and leave.

I am slipping. I need to tie up my loose ends. The first thing on the agenda will be to

handle things with John. I don't like that he feels like he has something to hang over me. All

that shit he talked about going to the police messed up our working relationship forever. As

detrimental to his health a decision like that will be, this stupid motherfucker just might do it. I

make plans to handle that situation ASAP.

Craig:

I can't prove it, but my gut is telling me that Ben is somehow behind Cynthia getting shot. I've been hitting the streets hard. Each time I try to connect the dots, I end up at a dead end. I feel like killing Ben just out of principle. I would have killed him two decades ago, right along with his wife and brother Brian. Ava saved his ass. She was right though. She came up big time with blackmailing Ben. Money wise, she is straight.

She doesn't need his money anymore. She's making money. I'm itching to kill that baby daddy of hers. She and I may need to sit down and talk about this again. If I find out he's behind Cynthia's coma, there's no amount of pleading Ava can do. I'm killing him. That's a promise. I might kill him anyway.

Every day, I'm at this hospital praying that Cynthia wakes up. Anytime her eyelids flutter, my heart races. Each time, I hope her eyes are going to miraculously open after they flutter. I'm losing hope. I know that's not good. If she were conscious, she'd be the one telling me how important it is to remain positive. That stuff sounds good, but I deal with real life. Real life is fucked up. Plain and simple. Shit's more likely to go bad than go good.

Life is full of disappointment. I conditioned myself to stop expecting good things to happen. The last time that I felt like life could potentially be taking a turn for the better, I got a rude awakening. It was a few nights before Evelyn was going to take off to start her freshman year at UMass. I figured my commute to see her at UMass would be a hike, but she was worth the trip. We kept our shit a secret, but we were in a relationship. At least I thought we were.

She called me up. She said that she was stressed and anxious at the same time. She asked me to come over and make love to her. I did exactly that. I made love to her. I loved her. So many times, I wanted to tell her. I told myself that I was going to tell her that night. I never got the chance to. When we were done making love, she started talking about what life would be like for her once she leaves. Not one time, did she mention me being a part of her new life. In fact, she said that she was going to miss our arrangement and thanked me. Yooooooooo, she thanked me for the dick like I was providing a paid service. I played it off like I wasn't hurt, but I was

. On that day, I gave up believing that good things are likely to happen to a man like me. Good things happen to other people. Evelyn was too good for me. When I met Cynthia, her spirit reminded me of Evelyn. She is such a positive person. She makes me feel good about myself, the way Evelyn used to. Then unthinkable happened. Evelyn got killed. Now Cynthia might not make it. God is definitely punishing me.

"Cynthia, wake up baby . . . I need you."

Karma:

Ray is opening up some more gyms in other states along the east coast. He's been away from home more than usual. I'm ok with it because more gyms means more money. I can entertain myself while he's away. I will admit, at first I was getting a little irritated. He'd travel for a four- or five-day span and come back tired. He didn't want to do anything except rest. He

didn't want to fuck. He was acting like an old man.

Once this started becoming a more frequent occurrence, I start doubling up with my JV

team. I am doing them daily. Ray leaves and I make plans with all three of them. I tried to be

good and just do one of them at a time. That didn't last long. There are days when I do all three

of them at different parts of the same damn day.

I am addicted to sex. I know it. So far, it hasn't presented a problem. I'm hoping that it

never does. Ray is gone too often for me to hold out and wait on him. Even when he is home,

he can't quench my thirst. Two times in a day isn't going to cut it for me. Three to four times

will suffice. No one man can handle that. That's why it's imperative that I keep three more on

the side.

Ray tells me that his cousin is getting married and he is going to be in the wedding party.

He says that he'll be sitting at a table with the wedding party. Ray suggested that I invite a

girlfriend to come with me. This way I won't be sitting alone. I tell him that I know exactly who

I'll invite.

"Hey," I say all extra loud.

"Why are you hollering?"

"I don't know. I'm hyped, I guess."

"So, what's up?"

"Since we are best friends now; do you want to go to a wedding with me?"

"Not really."

"Oh, yes you do, bitch" I say smiling through the phone.

"I can hear your excitement through the phone. There must be another layer to this invite."

"Ray's in his cousin's wedding. The cousin you had a run in with at their family reunion. Well, that hoe is getting married. Ray's in the wedding. So I get to invite someone to attend with me. If Ray's in it, I'm going to trust my gut that Richard will be in it. If he's not in it, he'll definitely be in attendance."

"Are we going there to play nice or act a fool? I gotta know so that I pick the right outfit."

"You are sooooo stupid!" I say laughing.

I tell Eve that I will bring in the wedding invitation as soon as Ray gets it. I knew she'd be down with going. This is the perfect opportunity for her to see what Richard's been up to and let him see what he's been missing. I know she's probably planning her outfit right now. Shit, I would be too. There's nothing like a going-to-see-my-ex outfit. That's always the sexiest dress you have in your closet. Sometimes it's not even in your closet. Sometimes you gotta go to the store to get it. It's all in the name of looking better than the new bitch. I can't wait!

I have been staying at Ray's for some time now. I've unofficially moved in. There was no

conversation about moving in. I just stayed over one night and never went back home. Ava isn't

feeling this. She left me a voice message saying that I gave her no notice whatsoever. She said

that I was getting to be an inconsiderate spoiled little bitch. She also said that since I thought I

was grown enough to move in with a man, he could take care of me now.

I am not sure what that means. Does this mean that I am not getting any more money? I

know that Ben is still sending checks. Mom usually takes her cut and deposits the rest into my

account. Is she saying that I am no longer going to get my portion? She better not be talking no

stupid shit like that. I call her up after I listen to the message.

"Hello"

"Is this my inconsiderate-I-think-I'm-grown-now daughter?"

"Hi Mom," I say with a slight attitude. Actually, it was a major attitude. This bitch is

holding my money like ransom for the return of her daughter. Why would I move back home

with my mother and my grandmother? What young adult would choose to live like that if they

don't have to? My mother and my grandmother are always fighting. They both talk shit to each

other and about each other.

I don't know who is worse. They both use vulgar language like English is their second

language. I thought my mom was bad, but my grandmother gets down and dirty right with her.

One night, as I was at home getting ready to head out to the club, I was blasting a rap mix on my Dr. Dre speakers. It's old-school rap from the 2000s. I get a knock at the door. It was more like pounding rather than knocking.

Bam Bam Bam Bam Bam! My door is vibrating.

"Yaaaaaaah!"

"Karma turn that rap shit down. I don't wanna hear about no dude slurping on somebody's pussy while I prepare dinner!"

Just as I turn down the music, my grandmother walks by and adds her two cents.

"All *you* do is let men slurp on your pussy, Ava. I'm not sure why you're uncomfortable with your daughter's choice of music. I'm surprised your hoe-ass ain't up in there with her shaking your ass."

My grandmother was smooth with it. She said it in a matter of fact type of way. She didn't say it with an attitude or anything. She said it with the normalcy of saying something like "Pass me the salt and pepper please." Then she walked away.

Ava wasn't having it. As my grandmother smiled walking down the hall, my mother went in on her. She didn't walk down the hall and follow her. She yelled like she was in an argument with a cheating lover.

"You old ass bitch. You're upset because men still want to slurp my shit. For the record, they eat my ass too. Raggedy, dry-pussy bitch. Keep talking shit and I'll put you out this bitch! Keep playing with me." Ava doesn't play. She'll cuss her own mother out just as quickly as she would a stranger. I tried to stay off of Ava's bad side. I heard that Ava was worse when she was

my age. I can't imagine there being a worse side than this.

Eve:

I hear about a boat cruise that's going to be held on the Spirit of Boston. Tickets are one

hundred dollars for VIP. I want to go, but I don't have anyone to go with. Neal has plans. I

already asked Karma and she said that she has plans. I wonder what plans she has because Ray

is out of town again, so they can't be plans with him. I'm going to leave that one alone.

I tell myself the only way I'm going to meet new people is if I go to social gatherings. I go

on Eventbrite and order my ticket. I purchase one ticket in the VIP section. At least I know that

I'll have a seat to sit down at in the VIP section. Going by myself was not the original plan, but

I'm ok with it.

I walk to one of the Asian convenience stores. Once I'm inside, I look for hot tamales

candy in a bag instead of in a box. Trial and error has proven that the candy in the box get stale

and hard faster than the candy in the bags. I stay away from the boxes if I can help it. There's

one bag left! You'd think I just hit the lottery or something. I grabbed the bag down off of the

rack and had a huge grin.

The cashier doesn't look me in the eye. She's a short Asian woman. I can smell her

breath from the other side of the counter. Her breath smells like fish. She needs to pop a few mints. I feel myself getting an attitude, because she's making me feel insignificant. Why can't

she just look at me when she's talking to me? As my attitude creeps up on me, my inner-racist

self is trying to creep in too.

I'm thinking of all types of racist shit to say to her. I'm looking at her high-water elastic-

waist, baggy jean pants that are two sizes too big. She has a short-sleeved button-up pink and

orange polka dot shirt with two pockets in the front. It look like she got it from the Salvation

Army. I can't see what she has on her feet, but I'm sure I won't be disappointed. Curiosity kills

me. I lean forward to see what she has on. Motherfucking jellies!

She takes the money for the candy. I grill her. If she was looking at me, she would've

seen that I was giving her direct eye contact. I zoom in and notice that what I thought were gray

roots at first glance are actually a shitload of dandruff. Ok, so now I'm grossed out.

Before handing me my candy, the cashier picks her nose real quick on the sly. She tries

to hand me my candy. I don't want that shit. That's one nasty woman. How could she pick her

nose and not think twice about it? Then she expects me to take my purchase. I want nothing

more to do with her or the hot tamales I've been craving.

When I don't take the hot tamales, she finally gives me the eye contact she failed to give

me in the beginning. I tell her that I don't want the hot tamales. She tells me to take them

because I paid for them. I scrunched up my nose, because her breath is kicking! Again, I tell her

no thank you and start to turn around and walk out. She scratches her dandruff and it looks like

somebody sprinkled instant potatoes on the counter. She wants to give me my money back. No

thank you! I am leaving without my money and without my purchase. That chick is too fucking nasty for me. I'm never going back to that store. Who knows what's all over the packaging, tons

of boogers and dandruff probably.

I decide to get some food since my temporary sugar fix gets nixed. I head over to the

shop that sells friend chicken and patties. I have a taste for a cocoa bread and cheese chicken

patty. I got put on to this when I moved to Boston. I don't know if Charlotte has a shop that

sells them. If they do, I have never been to one. I'm hooked.

Everyone in this shop is friendly. A West Indian family owns the shop. They wear hair

nets and plastic gloves. That put me at ease. I am very comfortable eating here. There's a new

person taking orders at the register. While I wait for my food, another customer starts cussing

out the cashier. I didn't see it. Apparently, the cashier is trying to help out with getting the

order and she handles the customer's food with the gloves she had on while taking the money.

I feel bad for the cashier. I know that she is new. She's young too. The customer tells her

that she better have someone else give her some new corn bread before she acts like a fool.

The cashier apologizes. I feel the customer. Dollar bills are disgusting. There's no telling what

germs and diseases are on them. While the cashier has someone else get a piece of cornbread

for the customer, she calls my order. It's done.

I'm thinking about how good this patty is gonna taste. It smells so good. My hand is hot

from holding the brown paper bag it's in. I can already taste it. As I'm walking out of the shop, I

notice that everything looks clean. The floor is clean. The brown lunchroom tables are wiped

down and the trash bins don't have food spilling out of them.

161

I had too many things in one hand. I dropped my car keys right next to the threshold. When I attempt to pick them up, I screamed on the inside. A big-ass light-brown roach runs across my keys. I'm fucking grossed out. I don't even want to pick up my keys. I use napkins to pick them up and throw my patty in the trash. Who knows what was running around in the back where they prepare food! I'm not chancing it. This is definitely not my day for food!

The party on the boat is tonight. It's a baby-blue themed event hosted by Afrique Events. I've gone on their web page and viewed some of the pictures from previous cruises. It looks like everyone is having a good time. It isn't until this moment that I realized the majority of the people the boat will be African. I guess I should have known from the name, but I just figured it would be regular black people. I didn't grow up around many   Africans in Charlotte.

Boston has a significant population of Africans from many different countries. Boston is more diverse than I thought it would be. I'm looking forward to being around a bunch of black people. In Charlotte, that's all that I was around. In Boston, that's not the case. I must say that it was difficult to find a baby-blue outfit. I had to rush order something online. I bet all of the Africans will have on some afro-centric shit from their country, dashiki's and shit.

I bought a baby-blue and white shirt dress from J Crew. I'm sure I won't see anyone with my outfit on. To most, it probably looks really plain. Females will be on this cruise trying to outdo each other. That meant the shorter the tighter the better. I am not looking for any attention tonight. Believe me, I can compete with the best of them. Tonight, I will be there to observe, have a good time and possibly meet some new people.

Thank God I bought a VIP ticket. The VIP tickets allow you to skip the line. The line to board the Spirit of Boston is intimidating. It is all the way down the street. Although it is nice out, I still don't want to wait in a line. I am by myself. Who wants to wait in a long-ass line for a party by themselves? Do people even go to parties by themselves?

Once I get into the VIP section, located on the top deck, I am greeted by a white hostess with champagne. I take my glass and laugh to myself. I like that a white person is serving all of the black people. Black people have been serving white people forever. I don't know if this choice to have white servers was strategic or not. Regardless, I still give the person in charge two thumbs up.

I'm part of the first group of people to arrive in the VIP Section. I have my choice of seating. I decide to sit in a spot away from where people will be dancing. I need a spot where I can see everything that's going on. I also need to be close enough to the exit in case some shit started popping off. I know that I can't leave the boat, but I can get the hell off of this floor level if things get crazy.

So far so good. I've been here for about an hour. The music is good. The dance floor is packed. Nobody has acted up. The only thing I'm missing is a partner to kick it with. As soon as that thought enters my head, this chick comes and sits where I am sitting. There are other seats. She doesn't have to sit next to me. For some reason, she does. I acknowledge her. I give her a quick smile and go back to people watching.

"How ya doing?" she says after I give her the acknowledgement smile.

163

"I'm good." I go back to people watching.

"I came here by myself too, but I knew I'd see people I know. I've noticed you sitting here by yourself. None of your girls have come over. I figured, that must mean that you're here alone too."

She sounds like a dude trying to pick me up. "Yes, I'm here alone," I say and smile.

"I'm B.J."

"I'm Eve. Nice to meet you."

B.J. talks my ear off for the rest of the night. She is nice though. She is funny as hell. I am still trying to catch her angle. She is very pretty, but in a low-key type of way. Her lipstick is a nude color. She had on blush, mascara and eyeliner. Her brown hair is pulled on the top of her head into a bun. The bun is big and full. It look like it is her hair. She works out because you could see the definition in her arms, back and shoulders. She has on baby-blue slacks, three-inch open-toe wedges and a white tube top. The only pop of color that she had is her bag. It is a red and white polka dot clutch bag. Her outfit is cute. I'll give her that. Her earrings are dope. Both earrings go all around the perimeter of her ear. It is one piece but it gives the illusion of her having about twelve solitaire earrings from the top of her ear to the bottom of her earlobe.

As I was admiring her earrings, three chicks come and stand right in front of us. My view is obstructed and my mood becomes sour. In my most kind voice, I ask if they will scoot over some. They are all drunk. The acted like they don't hear me or cam care less. I ask the slutty-dressed ring leader directly this time. She whips her cheap ass weave around in a dramatic fashion. She whips it a little too hard and loses her balance, trying to be cute and shit. As she

attempts to steady herself, she spills her drink all over my baby blue outfit.

I am not there with my girls. I know it was an accident, but I am still pissed. I

contemplate my next move. As I am contemplating, her two stooges start laughing. It is that

irritating drunk laugh. I am ready to throw down now. Bitches play too much. Drunk or not,

somebody is catching an ass-beating tonight. It is a three to one ratio. I don't care.

BAM! I punch the hoe in her overly made-up face. Her two girls try to jump in. B.J. jumps

in and helps me out. Now the ratio is two to three. The odds are now better. B.J. can hold her

own! She knocks out one of the stooges with the first blow that she delivers. The other stooge

gives her a run for her money. Once I beat the clumsy hoe down, I jump in and help B.J. out.

Luckily, security has already left the VIP section to do rounds on the floors that paid general

admission.

Nobody jumps in to break it up. Folks just stand there and watch. Some record it on

their phone. After it is over, B.J. and I leave VIP and go down to the first floor. We decide to get

on the dance floor to dance and blend in. Fifteen minutes before the boat makes it back to

land, security comes to the dance floor. Two white guys dressed in hoodies escort us off of the

dance floor. Somebody obviously dropped a dime on us. Security detains us for the rest of the

night and advises us to never show our faces at an Afrique Event.

B.J. had gained a lot of respect from me. She didn't know me, yet she held it down for

me. I came in solo and left with a new partner. Too bad we were banned from future Afrique

Events. I genuinely had a good time until those sloppy-sauced bitches fucked up my night. I lo on the bright side. They could have had me arrested. Lord knows that I don't need any more

run-ins with the law. B.J. and I exchanged contact info and go our separate ways, once they let

us off of the boat. What a night!

Bitter Endings

Craig:

This motherfucker thinks he is slick. I knew he was behind this shit! This is why I always

tie up loose ends. I never underestimate people. I usually don't leave anyone alive that may

want to retaliate. That's not how I handle business. Ben is still around because of Ava. She

saved that fool's life. He's gonna pay for this one though. His baby mama can't save him this

time. Always trust your gut.

I'm gonna wait for things to die down some. The police are still investigating. I'm a

patient man. I will get him when he least expects it. He won't know that I know he's behind this.

I'm gonna keep that piece of information to myself. I got something for his ass. John is being

taken care at this very moment. He gave up all the information that I needed. Ben almost got

away with this shit. Thanks to John's rat ass, Ben is going to get what he deserves. He's gonna

pay for what he did to Ava all those years ago. He's also gonna pay for what he did to Cynthia.

He really has no idea how evil a motherfucker like me can be. I got a lot of displaced anger

waiting for his ass.

Karma:

Eve asked me to go on some African Cruise, but I have plans. Ray is going to be out of town. I need my fix. I plan on seeing all three of my men tonight. I book three rooms at the Marriott, because I don't want to risk them running into each other. I am tired of going to their homes. I need a change of scenery. I book each room on a different floor. I am meeting all of them tonight. I schedule in two hours with each of them and carve out a half hour to recover and regroup.

I'll be starting off with my Latino Licker. He spends the most time eating it. He knows my pussy just as well as I do. I can't have him licking my pussy back to health after I let somebody else beat it up thirty minutes before him. So he will be first.

Next, I will hook up with Lip Service. That West Indian or Haitian, can really talk some good shit. It never takes long for my panties to get wet with him. I'll give him some head and he'll forget all about returning the favor. That man knows how to put it down. I should really give myself an hour of recovery time with him before I move on to School Boy.

School Boy is my bitch. He doesn't know it though. He does whatever I say. If I tell him that he better not take his mouth off of my titties, he does as he is told. School Boy doesn't dare move until I tell him to. Even after he climaxes, I make him ask permission to withdraw. That's just how I like it. The other two like to tie me up, but will never let me tie them up. School Boy lets me. I am thinking of asking him to get one of his friends on the basketball team to join in on our fun. There's one that I've noticed catch a woody whenever he sees me with School Boy. I'm hoping they are both down, because I want two men at the same time.

Tonight will be a busy night for me. Did Eve really think I'd pass up three dicks for a boat ride around the Boston Harbor? To be fair, she didn't know what my plans were because I didn't tell her. We are becoming cooler and cooler each day, but I keep my personal shit to myself. I never tell anyone everything about me. That's one thing Ava taught me that I agreed with wholeheartedly. Never trust anyone with all of your business.

After a long night of sexual escapades, I'm tempted take my ass home to my mom's house. I feel a tiny bit of guilt. It's almost enough guilt to make me not go back to Ray's house tonight. I'd rather sleep in a bed that's familiar to me than stay at a hotel. I decide to go to Ray's. I figure since he is out of town, I won't have to face him. I did some nasty things tonight.

When I get home, I'm shocked to see Ray's car in my driveway. I'm tempted to turn right around and go back to my mom's house for the night. That thought quickly evaporates. Things are that bad that I want to go back to my mom's house. When I enter his house, Ray is sitting in the kitchen chomping on Doritos and drinking root beer. He's not usually a junk food eater. This is a dead giveaway that he's stressed about something. I assume it's work related.

Never would I have guessed that he was pissed at me! I walk into the house exhausted, but I front like I'm not. I don't want any questions.

"Hey Babe!" I say all chipper and shit.

"Hey babe nothing. Where the fuck were you?" He says this with a calm yet stern voice.

"I was all over the place tonight, babe. Why are you swearing?"

"You were all over the place or all over someone else's dick?"

"What type of question is that?" I say a little too loud for his liking.

This maniac gets out of his chair all quick and shit and comes directly into my face. He's close enough to kiss me. I try to de-escalate things by kissing him because he's tripping. Next thing you know this motherfucker is biting my lip. He won't let it go! If I pull away, I will definitely fuck up my lip. He was biting me so hard that I knew he was going to leave teeth marks. That's when Ava's daughter surfaced. If he wanted to bite my lip it was gonna hurt him just as much as it hurt me. I managed to successfully form a lougie. I let it seep out of my mouth like foam. Once he felt that he released my lip, but not before calling me a disgusting bitch. Ava taught me well.

I don't remember seeing him backhand the hell out of me, but I remember how it felt. It felt exactly like how it looks in the movies. It stuns the shit out of me and puts me on pause for a minute. I took that minute to regroup. It actually took about ten seconds for it to sink in that I just got backhanded. There's no way that his hand didn't leave a mark on my face. He hit me so hard that I bet the veins in his hand are imprinted on my cheek.

Ava didn't raise a punk bitch. As much as I tried to distance myself from my mother and her crazy ways, I am just like her. Ava didn't take shit from anyone: man, woman or child. She didn't play and she taught me not to play either. I haven't had to flip out too many times in my life. When I do flip out, I flipped all the way out.

I've never been hit by a man. I'm angry and I'm disappointed. My reaction must have thrown him off. After I recover from the backhand to my face, I walk to our room and lock the door. He must think I'm in here crying. He's crazier than me if he thinks that. I'm plotting my

next move.

In the meantime, he's on the other side of the door talking shit. Telling me that there's

nowhere for me to hide or do sneaky shit. He has eyes all over. He asks me how I think he

knows about the men I just slept with. He said men and not man. So, he definitely has a good

source. Then, finally, he reveals that shady-ass bitch that checked me in at the Marriott

dropped a dime on me. She must want the dick. If she doesn't, most bitches would've just

stayed out of it. They wouldn't tell the dude.

I make a mental note to fuck that bitch up soon. She deserves it. Her nosey, big-ass

mouth got me my first beating by my man. I can't stay with a man that beats me. I don't want

to go to jail for doing something crazy to him. I plan my exit. My exit is going to hit him hard.

He's going to jail tonight for doing something crazy to me.

Since he liked to have people around him that drop dimes, I'm going to follow suit. He

bit my lip and backhanded me. That was more than enough of a reason to call the police. I look

over at the night stand. There's a halfway eaten piece of pizza with a fork and a knife beside it. I

look for two towels. Once I locate the towels, I use one and pick up the knife with it. I then put

the other one in my mouth to muffle my scream. Ray will now meet Ava's daughter Karma.

I take the knife with my left hand and grip the handle with a towel. With the other towel

stuffed in my mouth, I brace myself. I then hold my breath and stab my right hand in the meaty

part of my palm. It lined up directly with my pinky. That shit hurt like a motherfucker! I then

called 911.

Ray was still outside of the door running his mouth like a bitch. He had no idea how his night was going to end. He thought he won. Fuck him. He's going to jail tonight. Less than ten minutes later, the police are outside demanding that Ray open the door. My hand hurts like hell, but I'm snickering. Once Ray lets the police inside, they take him down. Ray's handcuffed and taken outside into a cruiser.

I have a handprint on my face, my lip is bloody from the bite Ray gave me and my hand is bleeding. The EMT showed up shortly after the police did. They take me to the emergency room. There the police take my statement.

"I came over to break up with Ray. He'd been sneaking around with a hotel clerk and I wanted nothing to do with him. Once I told him that I knew he was cheating on me, he went crazy! He tried to kiss me, but I didn't want his kisses. So he got a hold of my lip and wouldn't let go. He bit me! When he stopped. He dared me to say that I didn't love him. I told him that I didn't. How could I love someone like him? I shouldn't have said that. He became angrier and he backhanded me. I ran into the bedroom and he took his knife out and tried to stab me. I put my hands up to protect myself. All that he got was a piece of my hand, but I think he was angry enough to kill me."

The two Irish Boston policemen took my statement and believed every lie that I told. Why wouldn't they? I was very convincing, Oscar-winning convincing. I had tears and shit. Being secretly ambidextrous paid off. Everyone knew me as being right handed. The police wouldn't ever suspect that I stabbed myself with weak hand, my left hand. My prints were not on the knife, because I used a towel to hold the knife. Ray's prints were on it from using it to cut his pizza. What dude uses a fork and knife to eat pizza? My stab wound looked like a defense wound. Who in their right mind would stab themselves and blame it on their man? Right? That would be crazy!

He's going to pay for hitting me and making me stab myself. The police take Ray to lock up. He won't be coming home tonight. He won't see a judge until tomorrow. By that time, I will be gone. Fuck him and his snitching-ass Marriott girlfriend. I won't lie, she fucked up a good thing for me, but she can have his hardly-want-to-fuck ass. I'm on to the next. I look way too good to be letting some man hit on me.

The next morning, I'm back at my mom's house. I decide to call Eve and tell her the crazy shit that went down last night. She loves a good scandalous story. After four rings she picks up. She sounds groggy. Then I remembered she went on that African boat cruise last night. She probably just went to sleep a few hours ago.

"Hello," Eve says in a scratchy tone.

"Yooooooooo Eve!" I say all extra loud.

"You do know that I just went to bed. Why are you yelling?"

"Last night was crazy!"

"You and I have very different definitions of crazy. What were you up to last night?"

"Well, yes, you are right, we probably do, but I know you'll agree that this is crazy."

"Listen, I'm too tired to be guessing. Are you gonna fill me in or what?"

I told Eve about all that went down last night. She couldn't believe that I was crazy enough to stab myself; especially to the point to where I needed stitches. I could see her mouth open through the phone. When I was done telling her what happened to me, she told me about her night. She beat some hoe's ass on the boat. She deserved it. She told me that some chick named BJ held it down for her. B.J.? What chick do you know goes by B.J. It sounds very masculine. She must be a dyke.

Eve sarcastically says that we need to scratch the wedding off of our calendars. I tell her that my invitation hasn't be revoked. We are still going. She can't believe that I am still going. Eve isn't passing up the opportunity to see Richard. I'm not passing up the opportunity to beat that Marriott bitch's ass if she show up with my man. I wonder if they are fucking.

B.J.:

I met this baaaaaaad bitch on the boat cruise last night. She looked so good that other chicks were throwing her shade all night. One went as far as to spill her drink on her. I was watching from afar. She spilled it on purpose. I knew that it was gonna be on. I didn't want my new friend to get her ass beat and ruin that pretty face of hers. I went to help her out.

My future bitch could throw down! I thought that I was going to be the one to shut shit down. She actually ended up helping me out. One of the girls started to get the best of me. Eve

173

jumped in and we both taught that hoe a lesson. I am really feeling Eve. I was hoping that she

would let me get to know her better.

Eve:

I invite B.J. and Karma over to my place for appetizers and drinks. We are going to have

a girls' night in. It will be a chance for the three of us to bond. I hope that Karma and B.J. hit it

off. Unfortunately, they hit it off too well. Both of them get bent off of the alcohol. I get drunk,

but I get tired and fell asleep. When I wake up, I see Karma kissing B.J., while B.J. is finger-

fucking her on my living room couch.

That was way too much for me. Since when is Karma into women? I got the feeling that

B.J. was into women, but I made it clear to her that I wasn't. Karma is really thirsty for sex. She

obviously doesn't care who's providing it. She's known B.J. all of one day and she already let her

inside her panties. Karma notices that I woke up and I see what's going on. She doesn't even

flinch. She looks me dead in the eye and keeps doing what she was doing. I don't want front

row tickets to this flick. I make my way to my bedroom and go back to sleep.

When I wake up, both of them are gone. What the fuck! The house is a mess. Nobody

cleaned up after themselves or bothered to put any of the food away. Half-eaten buffalo wings,

mozzarella sticks and nachos were on the table and on my floor. Did these bitches think I wanted roaches? I fell asleep before them. They were up eating and drinking throughout the night and figured they'd leave the mess for me to tackle once I woke up. I'm heated!

The wedding is today. Last night, Karma confirmed that she is still going. I tell her that I wouldn't miss it for the world. I knew what is going to go down, so I dress for the occasion. There is definitely the potential for a beat down to take place this evening. We are going to skip the wedding and show up at the reception.

This wedding is huge. There must be three hundred people at the reception. Karma and I stroll in unnoticed. Richard's family has serious money. People are dressed like they are at the Grammys! Chicks are competing with the bride up in here. All the men are in tuxedos. Eve and I have on simple black stretchy dresses. They were simple, but we made the simple look spectacular on our bodies.

The wedding party is seated at the front of the room on a raised platform. I can see Richard. Damn, he looks good. I get a chill just thinking about how he used to make my body feel. That thought quickly goes away when I see a bitch whisper something in his ear and then kiss him on the lips. Did my eyes just turn Hulk green? Jealousy is creeping up on me.

Karma gives me a nudge. I look in the direction she's honing in on. There's a table of ten, but only nine people are sitting at it. She said that was our table. I start to make my move toward our table and Karma nudges me harder this time. This bitch is irritating me with all this nudging. Karma then says that her seat is now taken. Then I start to catch her drift.

There are nine people seated at a table because Ray's new bitch took Karma's seat. My

seat is still empty. Karma and I stand over in the corner and assess the situation. We watch the

folks in the room. Less than two minutes later, my seat is now taken. Guess who sits at my

seat? The Whisperer is now sitting in the seat that was supposed to be mine. Richard and Ray

have both of their women sitting at our seats. I tell Karma that I don't want to get arrested

tonight, but I think we should beat their asses. Just as I say that, the servers passed out

champagne to everyone at their table.

Karma says let's go. I am confused. I thought we were going to act a fool in here tonight.

We've done nothing, but we rush out of there like we stole something. I've definitely been left

out of the loop. Once we get to Karma's car, I demand some answers. We accomplished

nothing tonight.

"I need to know what the fuck is your problem." I say with an irritated tone of voice.

"Why do I have to have a problem?" Karma says smiling. She then starts the car.

"Don't pull out of this fucking parking lot until you explain why I got dressed up just to

attend a wedding we only spend thirty minutes at. That was such a damn waste of time, Karma.

I had better things to do. Next time you want to waste time, call one of your other friends."

"Ok, I'm gonna need you to shut the fuck up and listen to what I'm about to tell you."

I'm not feeling her tone, but I shut up long enough to listen. I should have trusted my

new best friend. She has things under control. We pull off. We didn't go far. We just went to the other end of the building. Out of the back door came a chick dressed in a waitress uniform.

Karma hands her five one-hundred dollar bills. The waitress hands her two licenses.

Obviously, I missed a lot. Karma drives off for real this time. We head back to my house.

She asks if she can stay the night at my place. She didn't feel like dealing with Ava tonight. I

agree to let her stay for tonight only. I like coming home to an empty, clean house. This bitch

didn't like to clean up after herself.

Karma:

At the wedding, I noticed that I knew the waitress from the salon that I go to. She's a

booster. She's in there every Saturday with shit that she stole from the high-end stores. I've

bought a few things off of her. She doesn't sell knock offs. She sells the real shit. It just happens

to be stolen. When I see her working as a waitress at the wedding, I put my plan into action.

Not only did home girl sell stolen goods, but she also sold pills from time to time.

I catch up with her when she is on her way to the kitchen. I proposition her and she is

down. She slip the two sluts a mickey for me and steals their IDs. I need to know their

addresses. I have future plans for those hoes. I'm sure that they were damn near comatose by

the time Eve and I got home. If they didn't fall asleep while they were there, they definitely

would have behaved as if they were sloppy drunk. I'm also sure that this embarrassed the hell

177

out of Ray and Richard. The booster texted me and confirmed with a short video that the sluts

were fucked up! I couldn't help but smile.

I need to go home. I planned on going through Ava's personal surveillance stash that she

keeps hidden in her bedroom walk-in closet. Previously, I found her stash on accident while I

was looking for a bad-ass pair of heels to wear. This time, when I walk into the closet, I see that

she changed things around. Ava's definitely been shopping. I remember that she had the

surveillance gadgets in a boot box. I look around for the box. I can't remember the exact box

and there are a few boxes that look similar to what I can remember it looking like.

The first box that I open is the wrong box, but its contents are very interesting. I put that

box to the side and continue to look for the gadget boot box. Four boxes later, I find it. I pick

out the surveillance gadgets that I need and go back to the other box that I found. There are old

pictures of Ava before her face got fucked up. There are newspaper clippings from almost two

decades ago.

After I find the box that I'm looking for, I sit in that closet for an hour piecing an untold

story together from Ava's boot box. When I come out, I don't know how to feel. Should I be

mad at Ava? Should I be mad at Ben? Should I be mad at Uncle Craig? Eve definitely should be

mad at Uncle Craig. He killed her mother and sent her to live with a crackhead. Damn. That's

fucked up. Eve has no idea that her mother is not her mother. She has no idea that she has a

daddy that is still living. She also has no idea that her daddy is also my daddy. We are sisters.

Do I tell her? Would she believe me? Is it my place to tell her? Ava must know that she

hired her dead best friend's daughter. I hold the picture of Ava and Eve's mother, Charlene, at a coffee shop holding their babies. They were holding us. I also have Eve's birth certificate. We both have the same birthday, October fourth. Ben sure is a dog. He had two children by two best friends who conceived their baby on the same day. Ava's been keeping secrets. I took pictures of everything and put it all back the way that I found it.

Ava:

I have a long conversation with Eve. She said that she successfully completed the assignment. She figured out that Ben Ford is fucking Lance's husband. That is not what I was expecting. She gave me the proof and I couldn't dispute it. That nasty motherfucker. I'm sure Lance's husband had to know who Ben was. Ben may not have known who Lance's husband is, but Lance's husband knew Ben.

I'm torn now. Do I tell my best friend that my baby daddy is fucking his husband? Do I lie and tell him that he wasn't cheating to spare his feelings and emotional stability? What do I do? I think I need to have a conversation with his husband. He needs to leave Lance and let him live his life with someone new, someone that will treat him right. If I know Ben, he was hitting it raw dog. I don't want Lance ending up with HIV because of Ben's questionable sexual behaviors. I know just the right person to convince him to leave.

I thank Eve. I tell her that she can have a paid week off. I will have a new assignment for

her when she comes back to the office in a week. She was excited about the paid time off. I

could hear it in her voice. I hang up with her and make a phone call to Craig. We needed to talk.

"Hello" Craig answers.

"When can you meet me at Lynn Commons and have some ice cream with me?"

"I got a taste for some ice cream today."

"Let's meet there in at five p.m."

"Alright, you got that." Then he hangs up.

Craig knew that if I wanted to meet him for ice cream on the Commons that I had some

serious shit to talk to him about. He also knew that five p.m. really meant two p.m. Craig didn't

trust phones. He always assumed somebody was listening in. Whenever we scheduled a time to

meet over the phone we deducted three hours from the time we said. Craig is paranoid.

As usual, I get there before Craig. He always shows up five minutes after me. He sits

down next to me on the old bench. I'm sure some homeless person was on this very bench the

night before. He starts right in on his butter pecan ice cream. That was my cue to start talking.

"Lance's husband is fucking Ben. I don't want to devastate Lance by telling him that. He

suspects something's up. He hired me to confirm his suspicions."

"So how'd you find out?"

"I didn't. I put one of my new eager employees on it. She found out and reported back to me. Which brings me to something else I need to tell you."

"What? You hired Charlene's daughter to investigate her daddy?" Craig says snidely.

I'm caught off guard and shocked that he knows. "How did you know that?"

"It's my business to know. Why did you take so fucking long to tell me?

"You were so messed up about Cynthia and finding who did that to her. I figured why add to your already full plate. I was going to tell you, but I wanted to make sure you were in a better space before I did. "

"So, now you think I'm in a better mental space? Listen. We're fam and all, but I don't need you thinking for me. And I definitely don't need you keeping important information from me. How do you know that she didn't come back up here to kill whoever killed her mother?"

"She has no idea that her mother isn't Gina. She has no clue who I am or that you even exist."

"I know. I've been watching her. She doesn't know. Let's keep it that way. Especially because I'm going to kill her daddy. Lance won't have to worry about his man sleeping with Ben. Ben will be taking an overdue dirt nap soon enough."

Craig gets up from the bench and tosses his unfinished ice cream in the green metal trash can. The city must have just collected trash, because I can hear the ice cream cup hit the

181

inside of the can and then settle at the bottom. Craig walks away. He doesn't look back. He

doesn't say bye. I know he's pissed at me.

We are like brother and sister. It's been that way since we were young. We both had

each other's back. I never withheld information from him. I thought about why I didn't tell him.

The reason why I didn't tell him is because I didn't want him to kill her. She was the only piece

of Charlene that I had left. Craig's big on not leaving loose ends. I had to beg him and provide a

rationale in order to convince him not to kill Ben or Charlene's baby. He hurt me when he killed

Charlene. We were just getting our friendship back and he goes and kills her. I understand why

he did it. Had it not been Charlene, I would have no problem with Craig killing everyone in the

family.

Charlene and I go way back. We went through so much together. We had a fallen out

that lasted about a year. It was crazy. One day I went off on her. I was mad because she

cancelled a girls' trip that I was looking forward to. I'll never forget the anger that I felt when

she told me she wasn't going. I told her to swallow a razor.

After that, things went downhill. Next thing you know, I'm sleeping with my ex-

husband's brother Ben. Ben's sleeping with my best friend Charlene. She and I weren't talking.

Neither one of us had any idea that he was dicking both of us down. Then he marries her. He

rapes me. She and I have our babies on the same day. We connect the dots. She and I meet up

to attempt to rekindle our relationship. Things start looking promising. Then they change for

the worse overnight. Ben comes over to my house and throws battery acid in my face. Craig sees what he's done to me and kills Ben's entire family. He lets Ben live and gives his child to a

crackhead down in Charlotte.

Twenty years later and we are still dealing with old drama. I'm tired of the drama.

Speaking of drama, my mother is driving me crazy. She invited her old friend Rochelle over to

the house. I haven't seen her since I stabbed her with the scissors she used to chop off my hair

when I was in high school. My mom stopped fooling with her when she became first lady. Now

that she doesn't have her church anymore and her man is locked up, she's hanging out with

Rochelle's hoe ass again.

Every time that I come home, these two old-ass bitches are in my kitchen talking shit

and drinking my liquor. You'd never know that my mother is a preacher's wife. She has the

dirtiest mouth I've ever heard. Folks think that I'm bad. Let my mother get a few drinks in her.

It's over. Nobody is safe from her scrutiny! She even uses the word "cunt." I thought only white

people used that. I don't know any black people that use that. She did have a baby by a white

man. Maybe he used it.

My mother is talking about how Rochelle was back in the day. I overhear her telling

Rochelle about herself.

"Rochelle, remember when you thought you were the shit? Don't let you get a new

outfit!" my mother says laughing. She continues. "You were that bitch that you couldn't tell her

she didn't have it going on. And you loved the attention, good and bad. Remember when you

got that new leather jacket? You just got your hair done. You wanted to stop everywhere. You

wanted everyone to see how good you "thought" you looked! You were a mess back then girl!"

"Yes, I remember that. I also remember you going out to get the same jacket in a different color a few days later. I guess someone else was seeking attention too." Rochelle says sarcastically.

What is it about black folks that makes them not want to go home when they think that they look good? They want to stop by and say "Hi" to everyone. They run errands that they don't even have. My people kill me. We are a funny bunch.

Getting back to the drama, Craig's going to kill Karma's daddy. She's going to have a fit. I can't tell her. She won't ever understand why it's necessary. I don't want her to hate her Uncle Craig either. Poor Eve will never get the chance to know her biological dad. I feel awful, but again, it's all necessary. Ben stirred some shit up when he went after Craig's fiancé Cynthia.

He really loves Cynthia. He hasn't loved a woman since Evelyn. Craig thinks that nobody knows about him sneaking over to Evelyn's and doing her every chance he got. Evelyn figured that she was doing them both a favor by ending their sexual arrangement. The night that she told him that it was over, she told me that she really loved my cousin. She asked me to never tell anyone about their relationship. She said that she couldn't see herself worrying about a man like Craig. He was involved in too many things that risked him going to jail.

She gave them both a clean start. She went away to school and never called him again. He added more muscle to his hustle and became the man in the streets. I was pleasantly surprised when he introduced me to Cynthia. That meant something. Then he asked her to marry him. Life for him was looking up. Then Ben's hating ass goes and resurrects the demon in Craig by hurting Cynthia. I know that he was mad at Craig for killing his family. Ben knew the rules. He knew he was lucky to be alive. He should have left well enough alone. Now, he's really

gonna get what's owed to him. Death.

Karma:

I call B.J. over. That bitch could eat some pussy. I also call School Boy over. B.J. is getting

fucked by a dude tonight. She just didn't know it yet. I asked her if she is bisexual. She said she

isn't. I don't believe her though. Good dick will make you change your mind about only fucking

with women.

I have it all planned. I am gonna get her drunk and start teasing her. I think she gave up

on Eve once she turned her advances down. B.J. is just the extra something special I need to

add to my sex games. I open the door with a bra and thong on. I usually leave a trail of hair on

my cat, but today I shaved it bald. I had a feeling B.J. is gonna need some motivation. We are

gonna make a film tonight, except, I am the only one that knows this.

My mom has these old-school styled glasses that record video. I strategically place them

on a shelf where they'll go unnoticed and will still get a good angle for our adult film. B.J. is

drinking that brown liquor and licking her lips at me. She's sitting on the couch and I'm sitting in

my leather chair that's directly across from her. My legs are open wider than they need to be. I

start playing with myself. I'm thinking of things that will look good on camera. I can tell B.J. is

getting wet. She's squirming on the couch.

185

Then we hear a knock at the door. I know who it is. So I take off my bra and let my titties fall. B.J. can't take her eyes off of me. I open the door and it's School Boy. I tell him we are gonna have some fun tonight. He is gonna have a threesome. He gets to my house early. I guess he doesn't want either of us to change our mind.

B.J. is confused. She wonders what's going on. I order School Boy to sit on the couch next to B.J.; she makes this face like what the fuck. I tell her that I get turned on when people watch me engage in sexual activity. She says she's not with this and gets up to leave. I walk over to her and start kissing her with my and on her pussy.

Just as I expected, her pussy is soaked. It is going down tonight. I don't know if B.J. ever had dick, but she is getting some tonight. I lead her back onto the chair where I was masturbating. As I'm kissing her, I take her hand and put it on my pussy. My pussy was nice and smooth. I know she likes how it feels. Shit, I like how it feels.

School Boy is now on the couch stroking himself. The chair that I am on reclines. I lean it back and tell B.J. that my kitty wants to be licked. I tell her to take her clothes off so that I can have access to her beautiful body. At first she is reluctant because School Boy is here watching. I tell her to imagine that he's not here. I tell her that he's there for me. She agrees and strips.

Once she's naked, I order her to wet my pussy up. I take off my thong and push her head down on my pussy. Both of my legs are on each arm of the chair. She's on her knees making me weak with her head game. When I look up, I see that School Boy is naked and he has his condom on. He's ready. I motion for him to take B.J. from the back.

186

She has no idea that what she's in for. She's so into making sure that I'm pleased, she doesn't feel School Boy sneak up behind her. He takes her in one quick powerful thrust. She gasps and then screams. I try to call her down. She stopped licking my pussy and is as still as a statue. I tell her that it would really turn me on if she let me watch her get fucked while she ate my pussy.

I start massaging her shoulders one shoulder at a time because I have stitches in my right hand. I tell her to loosen up. I convince her that it will feel good. It will be the best sexual experience she's ever had. School Boy is dying to thrust in and out of her. I give him a stern look. He knows that means that he better not move. I give B.J. the rest of my drink. Then I put my tongue in her mouth. I tell her that's how I'm gonna move my tongue when it's in her pussy.

She loosened up some. I gave School Boy permission to start fucking her. He knows that he has to go slow with her and be gentle. He does just that. Once I hear the first moan come out of her, I know it's over. She's now my bitch. I have both of my bitches doing whatever the fuck I want them too. She is eating my pussy while School Boy is doing her doggy-style. I knew when it was feeling good to her because she started to be more passionate. She is hungrier. This is gonna be a great video.

Eve:

I bought a used red Toyota Corolla with my first few paychecks. Taking public transportation was fine, but not when you wanted to go food shopping. Taking a cab was getting old quick. The car was twelve years old. If I can get two years out of it, I will be grateful. It has just over one hundred and fifty thousand miles on it.

I drive out of the city to go to the grocery store. The grocery stores in Boston are too expensive for my budget. I go online and find a Market Basket in Chelsea. Their prices are right up my alley. I plug in the address on my cell phone and use the GPS on it to direct me there. When I pull up, the parking lot is packed.

What kind of sale are they having! It takes me fifteen minutes to find a parking spot. It is crazy! I enter the supermarket and think I enter a Latin country. Everyone is Hispanic. I know that there couldn't possibly be thousands of them in here, but it sure feels like it. I start to feel a little intimidated. Everyone is speaking Spanish. Shit. When I finish shopping and go to the register the cashiers are speaking Spanish too. I may be paranoid, but I think the cashier got an attitude when she realizes I don't speak Spanish and she has to speak English with me.

I push my grocery wagon out of the exit to my new used car. I smile. It feels good not having to rely on a cab to bring me home. If I want to stop somewhere on my way home, I can. If I want to go anywhere, I don't have to try to coordinate bus schedules or calculate how long it will take on the Orange line.

Once I put all of my groceries inside of the trunk, I unlock my door. I didn't need to because it was already unlocked. I know that I locked my door when I left to go into the store. Are you fucking kidding me! Some idiots broke into my car and stole my radio. People still do that? I was heated. They also took a TJ Maxx bag with clothes that I was going to return. I had the receipt in my pocketbook. They won't be able to get money for those purchases. They'll have to get a store credit for my stuff.

I start my car and say a prayer. All I want to do is scream and curse. If something bad could happen, it always happens to me. I'm reminded of my life growing up with Gina. Shit was always fucked up. I didn't know that she was a crackhead until I was a teenager. By tenth grade, Gina got off of crack. I don't know how she did it. She didn't go to a rehab. I remember coming home one day from skipping school. Gina was crying. Mr. Uncle had died.

When I heard the news, I can't say that I was sad. I was tired of him sliding is old slimy dick inside of me when Gina was out of it. There's no sense in telling a crackhead that her daughter is getting raped. That information would cause more harm than help. I was worried about social services finding out and taking me out of my home. Lord knows I should have been removed. I'd rather stick with the devil I know. So I let my mother's supplier, Mr. Uncle, hit it. In return, we kept a roof over our heads. I fucked him for rent money, food money, utility money and abortion money. I should have been buying birth control pills with some of the money.

When he died, I was afraid that we weren't going to be able to keep up with the bills, but it felt like a heavy weight had been lifted off of my shoulders. Soon after, Gina got her life back on track. She stopped smoking crack. She got a job and acted more like a responsible adult. I can't say that she acted like a mother. I felt like a burden most of my life.

I've just been all over the place. Neal and I still haven't hooked up. Our schedules keep conflicting. He better not be a disappointment in the bedroom department. I don't need him to have a gigantic penis to be able to please me. I just need it to be big enough to be able to slide in and out without coming all of the way out. I also need it to be able to hit the right spots. If he

can do that, we will be good.

He commutes to work every day despite the fact that he has a car. He says that it is

easier to take the train into work. I tell him that I will pick him up after work today and take him

to his house. He says that he can't thank me enough. I tell him that he can thank me with that

dick when we get to his house. He laughs it off, but I'm not joking.

I like that he is outside waiting for me when I pull up. He saves me the trouble of having

to find a place to park on this busy street. He hops in and gives me a kiss on the cheek before

putting on his seat belt. This is his first time in my car. I wait to see if he is going to say

something about the car. The phone rings and we both look at our phones. It's his.

The conversation was short and he gives a lot of one word answers. That definitely

makes me suspicious. I don't say anything, but I feel myself catching an attitude. It is nothing

that he said. It is everything that he doesn't say. He never says the name of the person he is

talking to. He is hiding something. He is definitely hiding something. It is too early for this shit.

Both of us are silent for the rest of the ride to his house. I pulled into a parking spot right

in front of his apartment building. He lives in Malden on Summer St. The orange line was

parallel to his apartment building. The Malden Center train stop was a two minute walk from

his place. Now I see why it was more convenient for him to take the T to work.

He gets ready to get out and looks at me. I can tell he is wondering why I'm taking so

long to get out. I'm not getting out. I have a funky attitude now. The phone call messed up my mood. I don't feel like spending the rest of my evening with him. He definitely isn't getting any from me tonight. It doesn't take much to rub me the wrong way.

"You coming in?"

"No, I'm more tired than I thought."

"Really? You seemed ok when you picked me up."

"Yah, it just hit me all of a sudden."

"That's some bullshit."

"Excuse me?"

"You heard me."

"Nig . . . Let me not call you that. Neal, watch how you talk to me. You don't know me that well."

"Say what's on your mind then, Eve." he says all smart like.

"I'm not gonna waste my breath. I'm beginning to see that you may not be worth my time."

"What is it with you? One minute you are hot and the next minute you are cold. You should have that checked out."

"Motherfucker, get out of my car and go call that bitch back that you were giving one word answers to."

He had nothing to say after that. He just shakes his head like I have the problem and has

the nerve to slam my new car door. I want to jump out of the car and follow him into the front

hallway of his building to cuss his ass out some more. He never looks back. Had he turned

around, he would have seen my middle finger saluting him. I can't believe that I was seriously

going to give him some. Thank God I didn't. I would have been so mad at myself. On to the

next. Fuck him!

B.J.:

I need to stay far away from Karma. She's like a drug. She'll have you doing all types of

shit that you normally wouldn't do drug free. I'm ashamed of the things that I did with her and

what's his name. That's bad when you don't know the dude's name that's hitting it from the

back. I haven't had sex with a man since the eleventh grade. And it sucked. It felt NOTHING like

what that boy put on me last night.

Ever since I came out to my parents, I haven't flip flopped. I've only dealt with women. I

will never forget that day, my "gay birthday." It was a Sunday. My parents and I just came home

from church. "Let he, who is without sin, cast the first stone." The sermon that day was based

off of that passage. I was definitely moved by the sermon. It appeared as though my parents

were too. On this day, I harnessed enough courage to tell my parents that I am gay.

I'm sweating and holding my breath. I'm nervous as hell. I feel genuine fear. Will they

kick me out? Will they disown me? Will they drag me back to church to be prayed over? Will

they love me any less? Will they be ashamed of me? I can't keep this in any longer. It is killing

me to play make believe every day of my life to spare my parents feelings. I feel like I've been

convicted of a crime and now I am waiting to be sentenced.

Before either of them say anything, their facial expressions beat them to the punch. The

look on my dad's face is one of disappointment. The look on my mother's face is anger. Neither

one of them look shocked. That's the look that I was expecting. I think that they already know

that I like girls. Their already knowing, didn't make me coming out any easier.

My mom is definitely angry. She is angry at me for speaking "that foolishness" into

existence. My dad is disappointed as if I told him that I was dropping out of high school. I look at

the both of them. Didn't we just leave church? They had to have known that disclosing this isn't

easy for me. My mom isn't trying to hear it.

"Hey, Mom."

"Hey nothing. What do you want?"

She wasn't making this easy. "I want to talk to you about something."

"Belinda Jean, I don't have any money for any new activities! So don't ask."

"Why do you always come at me with negativity? You have no idea what I am going to

talk to you about! Never mind now." I say and head back to my room.

"What are y'all arguing about now?" my dad says as he strolls into the kitchen to get a beer.

"Your daughter has a funky, little attitude as usual."

"I have a funky attitude?" I say as I return to the kitchen. "All I said is that I want to talk to you about something. Then you start going off on me about money. I didn't mention anything about money, but you copped and attitude like I asked you for a thousand dollars."

"Well, excuse me for jumping the gun!"

"See, Dad, I can't even talk to her. She's so rude. I thought she stopped getting her period years ago," I say snidely.

"You little brat. You better hope that you don't need any money from me any time soon!" my mother yells as if I'm down the street instead of four feet away from her.

"I envisioned this conversation would be difficult, but I haven't even told you what I want to talk about and we are already in a bad space."

I was going to be gentle with my disclosure, but since people in the room had their filter off, I decided that I'd just spit it out. "I'm gay. I like girls. I am a homosexual. I'm a lesbian. Your daughter won't be getting married to a man and procreating. I just figured I'd let you both know."

It wasn't fair to my dad for me to come out like that. But my mother deserved the harshness. She was the very bitch that she wanted to call me but called me a brat instead.

194

"Oh! So you're going to come into my face and tell me you're a dyke. Well, fuck that

shit. I didn't raise no dykes. If you think you are a dyke you better unthink it. We ain't gonna

have none of that nasty shit going on in this house. I thought I had to watch out for the boys,

but shit, I now see you can't be trusted to have girls in your room. Hanging around with all

those spoiled white girls got you thinking you are one of them. Let the little white girls fuck your

head up to think that it's ok to be this way. It ain't! And you better NOT go running your mouth

to anyone I know about your new dykehood! I'm not going to have you embarrassing me

because you want to rub pussies with other girls!"

"That's enough, Clara!" my dad screamed.

She had gone too far. I walked out of the room with nothing to say. My head was

pounding and my heart was beating like I just ran a ten-mile race. I was ready to run away from

home. Didn't we just come from church? From that point on, things were never the same with

my mom and I. She has been jealous of my relationship with my dad for years.

It's not my fault that I feel more connected to him. He's easier to talk to. He doesn't yell.

He uses an inside voice. He supports me no matter what. The night that I came out, he and I

talked about what that meant for me and what my life would be like going forward. He told me

that there were lots of people like my mother in the world and sadly I was going to have to be

prepared for that type of reaction to my proclaimed lifestyle.

I didn't tell anyone else in the family. It became our little immediate family secret. It

wasn't until I left high school and went to college that I came all the way out. The day that I had a threesome with Karma was my "gay birthday." How ironic it is that I got dick on the day I gave

up dick.

Karma:

I've been following the Marriott snitch since the day after Kay's cousin's wedding

reception. I know her routine. I know her likes and dislikes. I've been all through her trash. She's

an alcoholic. She spends a lot of time at local bars during the week. She also drinks a lot when

she's at home alone. She drinks liquor like its juice. With that information, I plan my attack.

The snitch is on her way out of Packy's. I am grateful that she isn't able to find parking

close to the entrance. I am across the street watching her. I am acting like I am on the phone.

She is too fucked-up to notice me. I have to make my move soon. The police would be

patrolling this area soon because the bar is going to be closing. There is a high potential for

folks to act up.

Dressed in black jeans, black hoody, black steel-toed boots and a black ski mask, I swoop

in on her. She doesn't know what is going on. When she sees me, she stops out of shock more

than anything else. It is in that moment of shock that I used my equally strong left hand and

punched her with all of my might dead in her gut, hoping to hit her liver.

That punch stuns her system and shuts it the fuck down. She can't move. She is

temporarily paralyzed from the immense pain. Then she falls to the ground. While she is down,

I kick her in her coochie. That's something Ava taught me. She told me that if I did that to someone that was messing with my man, they'd remember how painful it was and they'd think twice before doing it again. Then, I take her car keys and left her there. This dumb drunk-ass bitch was going to drive home. I did her and the other unsuspecting people on the streets driving a favor. I saved lives tonight by stealing her keys.

I walk back to my car with my ski mask in my hand. I don't want to bring any attention to myself wearing it on Blue Hill Ave at one in the morning. My next destination is to her house. She won't be there anytime soon. The cops will probably take her to a holding cell to sober up or to the hospital. There's nothing like punching an alcoholic in their enlarged liver right after they just had a night of excessive drinking. Ava taught me well.

I us her keys to open the back door to her place. With my gloved hands, I turn the knob and the door squeaks. I don't know why I am creeping. Nobody is home. With that realization, I walk into the house like I own it. I have to get in and get out. I am not afraid of mice, but roaches I can't fuck with. I have some mice with me that I bought for my non-existent pet snake to eat. I release a few in the kitchen cabinets and a few in her bathroom. The rest of them I put in the refrigerator. I'm not sure if they will die before she gets home. If they do, I'm sure it will be just as effective. She will get a good scare and if she's smart she won't touch any of the food in there. Hope she's not hungry when she get home.

If they survive, when she opens the door, she will get the shock of her life. I'd love to see her face when the angry mice jump out the refrigerator at her. My next stop is to her bedroom.

I have two bags of roaches. I didn't go to the store for these. I went to Mission Hill for these bad boys.

I want the kind of roaches that are hard to get rid of. I want the resilient roaches. I need a few pregnant ones too. I paid two hundred dollars for someone to fill two sandwich bags with roaches. They thought I was crazy. They took my money regardless. I have those filthy insects triple-bagged. I can't risk any of them getting out. One bag of roaches I empty onto her queen-size bed and then cover them up with the comforter. The second bag, I let loose in her dresser and her walk in closet. That should be enough to fuck up her week. Bitches really shouldn't test me.

She's going to come home to mice and roaches. She won't be able to eat because the mice will have attacked her food in the refrigerator and her cabinets. She won't be able to go to the bathroom because I left a few in there and shut the door. She won't be able to lay down, because there's a sheet of project roaches waiting for her on her bed. She also won't want to take any of her clothes in the dresser or closet because they are both infested with roaches. "Check Mate" as my mother would say.

Ben:

Things been kind of quiet these last few days. It's the kind of quiet that worries me. It is like the quiet before the storm. I just don't know what type of storm is coming. I can't shake this unsettling feeling. It's Monday, so, I decide to continue with my normal routine. It's almost time for my manicure and pedicure standing appointment.

I drive up to Lynn. It's about a forty-five minute ride from Milton. That's where I get my hands and feet done. I like to be up in the cut when I'm tending to self-care. I'm destined to run into someone that I know if I stay on the south shore. Nobody that I know goes to Ocean City Nails in Lynn.

As I'm getting my pedicure, I look over to the woman that is sitting to my left. Her feet look like they have triple knuckles. How do women's feet get so jacked up? I can't imagine a pair of shoes that nice that it's worth fucking-up your feet like this. I get disgusted and look at the woman to my right.

Her feet are no better. I feel bad for these Asian folks working on these jacked up feet. They have to talk shit to each other about their client's feet. I know that I would. This lady to my right has toe nails as thick as pound cake. How do folks nails get that thick! I know that there is nobody at her house sucking on her toes. If they do, they may come up with a mouth fungus.

When my nails get finished, I go in my wallet and tip the little Asian cutie the same amount of money that my nails cost. She takes extra care of me. I don't have to ask for the same person to do my feet. She won't let anyone else do them. She wants her tip and I want good service. So it all works out.

Next, it's time for my shave and line up. I head back to the hood for that. That's where I

keep up with my gossip. The barbershops are just as bad, if not worse than women's' hair

salons. Men talk all types of shit about shit that they know and shit that they don't know. I

leave out of there with all types of information. I know what info to take heed to and what to

purge.

What catches my ear is some gossip about Craig's lady. This one dude with an irritating

lisp says that he heard Craig's lady is brain dead. Another dude chimes in and says that he hears

she'll be a vegetable if she even wakes up from the coma. I get quiet and listen to folks go back

and forth. After about two minutes, I add my two cents and say that I heard that nobody has a

clue as to who actually did it.

Then the speculation and guestimations begin. Everybody has a theory, but nobody has

a clue. I am relieved. I leave the barbershop feeling good and looking good. I get into my

midnight-blue Infiniti SUV. I turn on Sirius Satellite radio station ninety-six and listen to The

Foxxhole. I'm just sitting and listening to the various comedians.

The bitches are funnier than the men. Sommore comes on. She starts talking about how

ghetto black people are. What makes it even funnier is that I can relate to everything she is

saying. I'm laughing so hard my stomach hurts. I reach for my phone and it is nowhere in sight. I

must have left it in the shop.

It's only been five minutes. As I'm walking back to the barbershop, I'm silently praying

that nobody got me for my Apple phone. I walk into Mattapan's Finest and my phone is exactly where I left it. Prayer works. I grab my phone and tell everyone goodbye for the second time. That would have messed up my day big time had my phone not been there.

I get back into my whip and something doesn't feel right. Something feels off, but I can't put my finger on it. I try to shake the uneasy feeling that I'm having. Next stop is to the crib. I need to unwind and think about my next move. Whenever I feel like this, something usually pops off. I may need to take an impromptu vacation. My phone beeps twice indicating that I have a text message. It's from Ava.

Ava:

My energy level has been low. My hair has been falling out to the point where I'm starting to look like a cancer patient. The little hair that I have left is doing nothing for my self-esteem. I've stopped getting weaves and have been wearing wigs. I'm too ashamed for anyone to see me at the salon, including my stylist.

I've been having joint pains in my hands. They are starting to look discolored. My hands actually look as if I took a gray crayon and colored it on top of my light skin. The only person that has noticed that I haven't been myself lately is Lance. He hasn't even seen me. He could tell by my voice that something wasn't right. If he seen me, he'd know something was up. I look and feel like shit.

My physician confirmed what I already knew. I'm sick. My labs confirmed that I have

Lupus. Just add that to the list of fucked-up things that have happened to me. Folks wonder

why I'm bitter. Let half of the things that I have been through in my life happen to someone

else. The average person would have thrown in the towel a long time ago.

I decide to keep my medical information to myself. I don't tell my daughter because

she'll just worry. I'm not telling my mother, because she'll find a way to use that info against

me. In time, I will tell Lance. I tell him everything. Well, I tell him almost everything. You never

tell all of your business to someone. My physician mentioned something about chemo drugs. I

tuned him out after he told me that I have Lupus. Speaking of drugs, I owe Ben a visit before I

get too weak to take care of our unfinished business.

I send a text message to Ben asking him if I can meet up with him at his place to talk. He

takes a while to respond. I figure there is some reluctance on his part. In the end, he agrees. He

doesn't even ask why. He knows it must be important because I haven't reached out to him on

a friendly basis in decades.

I arrive at his place and I get the chills. He still lives in the same home as he did when we

were fucking each other. That was back in the day! We used to get it in! Ben was one of the few

men that I've had in my life that could keep up with me sexually. The last time that I was in this

house was when I secretly recorded Ben and I having sex. I leaked the video and posted it on his

brother's, Brian, Facebook page. My ex-husband saw his brother doing me. I felt vindicated.

Ben was just a casualty of war.

Ben paid me back by raping me and splashing battery acid in my face. He should have died for that. I let him live. I had to think about Karma. She deserved to have both parents in her life. She deserved to know both parents even if one of them ain't shit. The feeling I had growing up without knowing my father really bothered me. It affected me negatively. I wasn't going to rob Karma of her dad. My mother did that to me.

"What a pleasant surprise!" Ben says sarcastically.

"Save the bullshit. We need to talk."

"Sounds like serious business Joan. Come in and have a seat."

I give him the finger. He started referring to me as Joan Rivers after having multiple cosmetic surgery procedures to my face. We sit down on his monstrous chocolate-brown leather sectional. Then I begin.

"I knew that you were a freak and had an abnormal appetite for pussy, but when did you add dick to the menu?"

His hands clench and his yellow face turns red. "What the fuck do you want, more money? I've given you and my greedy daughter more money than you deserve. Both of you are some greedy bitches!"

"This has nothing to do with money, Ben. It has to do with Lance," I say with an attitude.

"Oh! Your faggot bestie. What could I possibly have to do with him? I haven't seen him in years. It's probably been at least ten years since I've seen his bitch ass."

"You got his HUSBAND opening his mouth and ass for you these days. I need to make sure that affair ends!"

"So you know about that? He ran his mouth to you? I may owe him another beat down for telling my baby mama my business," he says with a smirk.

"Fool! He didn't put your business out there. Your daughter found out."

"How the hell could she know about that? The only two people that could have known is Lance's husband. For the record, I had no idea he was your faggot-bestie's husband. The only other person is this fly little honey with a sweet-tasting pussy that I unfortunately didn't get the chance to dip my stick in. She witnessed more than she should have. You couldn't have possibly found out from her. Anyway, tell your bestie that I've ended things with his boo. He was too messy and too clingy."

I immediately felt sick to my stomach. Did this fool just say a *"fly little honey with a sweet-tasting pussy?"*

"From what your daughter told me, she witnessed more than you would want out in the streets. And for the record, I'm not talking about Karma. I'm referring to your daughter Eve with the *sweet-tasting pussy*. Eve works for my firm. She was investigating Lance's husband because he suspected infidelity. I would have never imagined you'd be who he was cheating with. You are such a whore."

"My daughter Eve? What the fuck are you talking about, Ava!"

I tell Ben that Craig never killed Charlene's baby Evelyn. He gave her to one of his hoe's family members. Evelyn ended up living with some crackhead in Charlotte, NC. Evelyn, who is Eve, lived a very different life than her half-sister Karma. By the end of the conversation, Ben is visibly affected by what I revealed to him. He doesn't say it, but I can tell he is messed up about eating pussy that was of his own flesh and blood.

Shit! I am disgusted! I really believed that there is no other option for this man but to die. I am going to save Craig the trouble. Ben raped me, disfigured my face and impregnated my best friend at the same time he impregnated me. Ben had sex with my other best friend's husband, ruining their marriage. He is behind Cynthia's attempted murder. On top of all of that, he had oral sex with his own daughter!

This man doesn't deserve to live. He needs a taste of his own medicine. I am going to make sure that he gets it. I ask him if I can use his bathroom. While I am in there, I get what I need from out of my pocketbook. After all of these years, I am finally going to repay him for all of the pain that he has caused me in my life and my loved one's lives. And unfortunately for Ben, I'm still bitter. Payback is a bitch!

Tonight when he has his protein shake, he will ingest enough poison to shut his organs down, but not before feeling the effects of the same date rape drug he gave me twenty years ago. Let him experience what it feels like to be helpless and immobile. Then the pain of the poison destroying his vital organs will creep in. He won't even be able to bend over in pain. He will suffer and then die.

Craig:

Things haven't died down completely, but I don't give a fuck. Ava told me about Ben and his nasty-incest ass. He needs to be put down like a dog before anyone else gets hurt by his recklessness. Living a life of crime has afforded me the opportunity to be skilled in many resourceful areas. Tonight, I will be demonstrating my extensive skillset.

I think I'll stick to the same theme Ava and I used to fuck with his brother Brian all of those years ago. I'll leave a gift for him in his car. Better yet, I will leave a gift for him under his car. There will be no surviving this.

Ava:

Ben's dumb ass takes his eyes off of me long enough to allow me to slip some drugs into his protein shake. I asked for some bottled water. He was so rattled by the information that I gave him about his daughter, he absentmindedly allowed me to go into the refrigerator. He asked me to bring his shake to him. It was a wrap after that. Soon, he wouldn't be able to move his limbs.

I was going to leave. Instead, I decided to stick around to witness the drugs take their effect. I start having flashback of the night he drugged and raped me. I wanted to spit in his face. I'm going to do something worse. I'm going to piss on him the way he pissed on everyone else in his life. Except I am going to do it literally. As soon as I could tell that he is immobile, I start talking all types of shit.

Then I pull up my skirt and slide my panties to the side. I sit on his face and urinate. Fuck him! I get up and take his keys to his new Mercedes truck. I knew he kept money under his seat. I figure I'd go buy myself a pocketbook on him. I leave him there with piss on his face as I walk to his garage. The car recognizes that I have the key on me and it unlocks as I put my hand on the door. I open the driver's side door. I instantly feel an intense heat. The heat is so hot that it feels cold. It is indescribable. With this heat, a blinding light follows.

BOOM!

Javier:

He thinks this shit is over. Nobody humiliates me! Nobody puts their hands on me and gets away with it. I'm from the D.R. In the Dominican Republic, we don't call the cops on each other. We handle our own affairs.

One minute he tells me that he loves me and the next he's threatening my life. To think, I was going to leave my husband for this mentirosa! I should have never strayed away from my marriage. I wanted to adopt a child and Lance didn't seem like he was on board. I wanted us to

have a family. Lance was fine with the way things were. He started showing me less and less

attention. So I got the attention from someone else.

When I find out that Ben is cheating on me with a bitch, I mean a real bitch; a female, I

lost it! I showed up at the hotel and ruined their little hotel stay. What the heck is he doing with

a woman? Since when is he bisexual? That man is a homosexual. I don't know who he thinks

he's fooling. I wasn't the only one sucking and savoring dick.

He messed up everything. My husband is asking me for a divorce. The adoption agency

turned us down when Lance told the social worker that we aren't on the same page when it

comes to wanting a child. He started sleeping in the guest room. I haven't had sex since Ben.

Right now, I'm opening Ben's door with the key that I had made. I walk into the living

room and he's laid out on the brown sofa. He doesn't move. He looks like he's tore up. He had

way too much to drink. This will make things even easier for me. I get closer to him and he looks

at me with pain in his eyes or is it anger. He doesn't move. He just lays there looking at me

crazy.

I'm here for one thing and one thing only. He stabbed me with his dick and then stabbed

me in the heart by walking out on me. I'm going to return the favor, except he will never get

any of my good Dominican dick again. I get closer to him once I realize he is so fucked up that

he couldn't harm me if he wanted to. He must have taken something else besides Henny

because brown liquor doesn't do this to him.

I love this man, but I love Lance more. We need to make our marriage work. It can't

work while my heart still belongs to this asshole. I can't have the temptation around me; not if I

want to give my marriage a fair shot. I get close to him and lean in to kiss him. I pull back when

I'm hit with the strong smell of piss. Did he pee on himself? With tears forming in my eyes, I

take out my just-in-case-a-bitch-tries-me blade and stab him repeatedly in the heart.

My heart is racing like it's going to jump out of my chest. As I walk toward the door, I

catch a glimpse of myself in the decorative mirror hanging in the foyer. I look crazy as hell. I

have blood on my face from wiping my tears away with my bloody hand. I make sure not to

open the door with my bare hands. I use the handkerchief that I brought with me. It's dark out,

but I can see that one of his cars is fucked up! The Mercedes truck is burnt like somebody blew

it up. I'm not exaggerating. I didn't notice it on my way in. Ben lives out in the cut. He has a lot

of land and no neighbors for damn near a mile. Somebody could die on his property and

nobody would know.

When I get to my car, there's a note on my seat with Lance's handwriting. I know Lance

didn't come to Ben's house looking for me. I must have overlooked the note when I got into my

car and threw my jacket on the seat. That's why I didn't see the note until I get back into the car

from Ben's house. The note says that he's been following me and been having me followed. My

heart starts to race again. He knows that I am cheating, but don't know with who. Now he

knows that it is with Ben. He tells me that he was going to reconsider adopting a baby with me,

but that's off of the table now. He called me a messy whore. He said that I should now consider

myself single. He's going through with the divorce. Lance threatened to bust my ass if I set foot in the house tonight or any other night. He advised me to take up residency with my new boo,

Ben. He'll have movers deliver my shit to Ben's house.

"Motherfucker!" I say as I bang my bloody fist against my dusty dashboard. It would

have been nice if he told me this before I killed Ben.

Karma:

On my way out of the Marriott snitch's place, I have a brilliant idea. I have three

miniature surveillance devices in my bag from my mother's closet. Why settle for having to

imagine how the bitch is going to react, when I can watch it live! I plant a device in her

bedroom, in the kitchen and in her living room. The devices are connected to my phone.

Whenever there is any activity in the rooms where I hid the devices, my phone will indicate it

via text message.

She comes home the next morning in the same clothes she had on last night. This

bastard didn't waste any time moving on. My ex, Ray, brought her home. The snitch looked like

death. Some peace and relaxation is exactly what she needs. "Sorry bitch, you'll have none of

that tonight! Believe that!" I yell into the phone as if she can hear me.

I thought that her place would have been crawling with uninvited guests by the time

she got home. It isn't. I guess they are vampire-like roaches and rodents that don't come out in the daylight. I should have known better and been more patient. Project roaches are

disrespectful. They don't respect the daylight hours.

As I'm watching my man Ray kiss on my raggedy replacement, I see a mouse run across

the floor. Neither one of them see it. I'm glad that they can't hear me because I am cracking up!

I can't wait to see their faces when one of them gets hungry and heads to the refrigerator. My

prayer is that it will have a traumatizing effect.

The roaches slowly start to make their appearance. The two of them are still slobbering

all over each other. They are oblivious to what's going on around them. That is until one of the

mice cock blocks. If I could give that mouse a fist pound I would. "Good looking out!" I say to

the mouse though my phone.

They get off of the couch and head to the bedroom. As soon as she stands up, a dark-

brown mouse runs right across that bitch's foot. She screams at the top of her lungs and jumps

on back on the couch. Ray tries to calm her down. He tells her that it just a little mouse. He

promises that things will be alright. He says that he'll track it and kill it for her.

Ray tells his new boo to go to the kitchen and get some water to settle herself down

some. She does as she's told. The suspense is killing me. It probably took all of ten seconds for

her to walk to the kitchen from her living room. My eyes were glued to the phone. My heart is

beating fast with excitement and anticipation.

If I didn't witness it and have it on film, I would have never believed it. When she opens

the refrigerator, three mice jumped out at her. Two of them jumped right on top of her weave and get stuck in her curls. They were squeaking and trying their best to get out of her cheap

head of curly weave. She couldn't even try to get them out because the third mouse jumped

right into her mouth as she screamed. You should have seen the bitch trying to get the mouse

out of her mouth. I thought it was going to force its way down her throat. I never saw no shit

like that in my life. I wish I could put this on social media.

Ray ran into the kitchen to see what's. By then she gagged the mouse out of her mouth.

She wouldn't stop screaming. She kept swinging her head from side to side violently in an

attempt to get the mice out of her weave. This show is hilarious. I couldn't have planned this

any better. Her savior Ray made her hold still long enough for him to get the mice out of her

weave. She is hysterical.

He settles her down. Then he looks around her place disgusted. I bet he is wondering

what type of nasty ass-bitch lives like this. Maybe next time, he will rethink who he decides to

lay down with. I was going to give him a chance to get me back, but I changed my mind. I'm too

classy to be dealing with a dude that lays down with hotel clerks. Plus he put his hands on me,

The two of them leave after they discover that the entire house is infested. She keeps

telling him that she is a clean person. She never had a pest problem. She has no idea where all

of the mice and roaches are coming from. The sad part is that she is telling the truth. The more

she tries to explain things to him, the more he probably thinks that she is lying. I'd seen enough.

Check Mate! Next on my agenda is to talk to Eve face-to-face. I text her. She says that she'd be

over in an hour or so.

My bedroom mirror is doubling as a make-shift white board. I have newspaper clippings and pictures hung up on my mirror like I am investigating a serial killer on Criminal Minds. My mom went out last night and hasn't returned. I have no idea when she'll be back. My grandmother is home, but she is on the phone talking to Rochelle. Rochelle is a pretty funny character to me. My mother can't stand her.

"Damn, what's all that shit on your mirror?" Eve says when I lead her into my bedroom. She is chomping on UTZ sour cream and onion chips.

"That's why I called you over here. Usually, I have no problem delivering important information. Today, I find myself struggling. I tried to put things in chronological order for you. Hopefully, it helps you in answering questions you've probably had for your entire life."

"What type of stuff is up there that could possibly answer any of my life long questions? How do you know that I have any unanswered questions?"

"I didn't know until I started reading through all of this shit. I found it in my mother's boot boxes. She has no idea that I know any of this stuff. We can confront Ava about this when she gets home. For now, just take a minute and look through everything."

The entire bag of chips is gone by the time that she finishes going through my findings. Eve walks over to me and hugs me. She says that she is so happy to meet her flesh and blood. Although, her biological mom isn't alive, she has Ava to tell her all about her mother. After all, they were best friends. This response surprises me. I expect Eve to be pissed, but she seems happy. I know that if it was me, I'd be heated.

She never mentioned anything about Uncle Craig. He killed her entire family, with the exception of Ben. She never mentioned anything negative. I found that shit weird as hell. Nobody is that positive. I'm gonna have to keep my eyes on her. Eve leaves my place. She lied and said that she had somewhere to be. That hoe didn't have anywhere to be.

Eve:

I knew that shady bitch Gina couldn't be my mother! Thank God! It was really hard to accept that a mother could be so unloving, uncaring and irresponsible. I pick up the phone and call her. I want her to know that I know she's not my biological mom. I want to tell her that she made my life a living hell. I want to tell her that despite her poor parenting skills, I will still become an exceptional woman. I was going to say a "Phenomenal Woman", but she wouldn't have known the Maya Angelou reference.

"The number you have reached is no longer in service," the recording taunts me.

The phone is turned off, maybe I will have to pay Gina a face-to-face visit. I'm not keeping this inside of me. She's going to hear everything that I have to say. She's also going to answer all of my questions. I click on the American Airline app on my phone and book a flight for next weekend to Charlotte.

My ticket is purchased. I'm going out there on Friday night after work and returning on Sunday night. That's enough time to do what I need to do. I try not to be vindictive. I'm normally a calm person. I consider myself to be someone that you can reason with. For the time being, that calm, reasonable person is on leave. Evil Eve is in the building!

Let me digest this. "Because this Uncle Craig person killed my family and sold me to a crackhead, I've had a fucked up life." I say out loud to myself. From what I've learned about Uncle Craig, he's had a good life. It's only fair that he get to experience some of the pain that I've felt. Because of Uncle Craig, I let my own father eat my coochie. Because of Uncle Craig, I was left to fend for myself with a crazy crackhead. Because of Uncle Craig, I was raped. Because of Uncle Craig, I haven't had any healthy relationships with men. I can't keep a man. That's all because of Uncle Craig. "Well, Uncle Craig, since you like fucking-up lives by killing people's families, I'm going to kill your family. I'll let you live, because you let me live. That's the least I could do." I say out loud to myself.

I didn't expect it to be easy to get into Cynthia's room. I heard that she woke up from her coma. I knew that I had to get into the hospital to see her before Craig brought her home. His security is top notch. There's no way that I could sneak into his place and kill her. I'd have to do it today at the hospital.

Ironically, security at the hospital for Cynthia had become lax since my father Ben was killed. I owed it to my dad to finish what he couldn't. Craig will be excited to take his fiancé home today. He may show up early. I'm going to have to do this quickly. Get in and get out. I sign in as Karma.

The nurse walks into the room and asked Cynthia if she wants to visit with someone named Karma. She told the nurse that it is ok. When I walk in, she has a confused look on her

215

face. I am in disguise. I have a red wig on and dark oversized sunglasses. She can't talk because she still has a breathing tube down her throat.

"Be calm. I know that you don't know who I am. My name is Eve. Eve Ford. I didn't know that was my last name until recently. Now I know that you have no idea why I am visiting you. We've never met. I'm here because I have some information about your soon-to-be husband. I wanted you to know the truth about your fiancé."

I tell Cynthia about how Craig killed my family and sold me to a crackhead. I tell her about everything. She's visibly upset. I see a tear falling from her left eye. Another tear follows from her right eye. I don't know if she's crying for me or because she knows that she's not going to make it out of this hospital alive.

With tears in my eyes I say, "I want you to know that your man killed you. I'm just the vehicle that's carrying it out. I'd say I'll see you when I get to heaven, but I'm going to hell. Tell my mother Charlene "hello" for me." With that, I inject the same poison that was found in Ben's blood stream into her IV. There is a commotion outside. I peak outside the door and hear, "Code Blue!"

Everyone is heading over to a room at the end of the hall. I knew exactly who was in that room. It was all over the news. Security is tighter outside of that door. An eight-year-old little white boy was hit by an Asian woman that admitted to texting while driving. They arrested her at the scene. Call me racist, but I believe that Asian women are the worst drivers.

I was able to slip out of Cynthia's room unnoticed. My next stop is to the airport. I am tying up all loose ends. Gina's life depended on how she answered my questions tonight. If it came down to it, I'll be doing the community a service by killing her. Nobody will miss a crackhead. I laugh to myself. *To Kill a Mockingbird* was a big hit. I wonder how many people would read *To Kill a Crackhead*. As I'm laughing, I get a text from an unknown number.

It reads: Did you really think Cynthia's room didn't have surveillance?

B.J.:

I said that I was going to leave Karma alone, but she needs me. We spoke on the phone and she He mother and her father were killed on the same day. It was some crazy shit. Nobody could figure out what happened at that house. There were all sorts of rumors about what went down in Ben's house that night. Some people think that Ava killed Ben, but the police can't prove it. The police even questioned Karma about her whereabouts when her mother and father were killed.

Ben died due to multiple stab wounds to the heart. An autopsy was ordered and they found that he was poisoned too. The police think that he same person that poisoned Ben also planted the bomb in his car. If that is the case, Ava didn't kill him, because she wouldn't have gotten in a car to blow herself up.

There is some talk about Ben being homosexual and his lover killing him, but that is a stretch. Anyone that knew Ben Ford knew that he was a ladies' man. Ava may have a homosexual best friend, but nobody believed that she'd have a baby by one. So there goes that theory.

Karma is beside herself. She's talking all types of crazy shit. Her grandmother is the one that actually called me. She said that she got my number from Karma's phone. She said that Karma wasn't eating and wouldn't get out of bed. What she said next embarrassed the hell out of me.

"Her friend Eve is out of state. I don't know any of her other friends. I figured that you'd care about her well-being considering the last time that I saw you at this house, you were licking on my granddaughter's coochie."

Karma told me that her grandmother was just as bad as her mother Ava; I got to experience firsthand. After I got off of the awkward phone call with her grandmother, I raced over to Karma's house. I wasn't going to let her deal with the death of her parents alone. I'd be there for her. I loved her. I was going to show her that I loved her. Maybe she'd leave dick alone and cross all the way over.

When I get to her house, the door is unlocked. I walk up the stairs to her room. Like her grandmother said, I'd been to the house before. I hear what sounds like weeping. I pick up my pace rush to open her door. I may need to make an appointment for a hearing test. What I thought was weeping wasn't that at all.

I open the door and find Karma having sex with a man that I swear I've seen a picture of before. Yes! I'm positive that I've seen this dude before. I've seen him in a picture with Eve. Karma is fucking Eve's ex-boyfriend Richard!

Ava:

My life flashes before my eyes. There are so many things that I still want to do and experience. I want to see my daughter on her wedding day. I want to experience what it feels like to hold my first grandchild. I want to locate my father and ask him why he never came for me. I want to get to know my late best friend's daughter Eve. I want to see how far I can take Still Bitter Private Investigating Agency. Lance and I still need to take a trip out of the country to just relax.

A deep feeling of sadness consumes me. I regret not making amends with my mother. I am sorry that I never took the time to listen to her story. I never took the time to understand her, so that I could possibly forgive her. I remained bitter. Being bitter brought a lot of pain into my life. One negative thing after another happened to me because I wouldn't let go of my bitterness. I missed many opportunities to let go and move on. I thrived on vengeance instead of choosing to work through my pain. Now, I don't have a choice in the matter. I have so many regrets. The bright flash of light becomes dim and I leave this earth.

Still Bitter.

45376816R00124

Made in the USA
Middletown, DE
02 July 2017